LEROY COLLINS LEON COUNTY ...
3 1260 0119... W9-DJQ-927

Ghosts and Poltergeists

Fact or  Fiction?

Terry O'Neill, *Book Editor*

Daniel Leone, *President*

Bonnie Szumski, *Publisher*

Scott Barbour, *Managing Editor*

OPPOSING
VIEWPOINTS®
SERIES

GREENHAVEN
PRESS®

THOMSON
————*————™
GALE

San Diego • Detroit • New York • San Francisco • Cleveland
New Haven, Conn. • Waterville, Maine • London • Munich

© 2003 by Greenhaven Press. Greenhaven Press is an imprint of The Gale Group, Inc., a division of Thomson Learning, Inc.

Greenhaven® and Thomson Learning™ are trademarks used herein under license.

For more information, contact
Greenhaven Press
27500 Drake Rd.
Farmington Hills, MI 48331-3535
Or you can visit our Internet site at http://www.gale.com

ALL RIGHTS RESERVED.
No part of this work covered by the copyright hereon may be reproduced or used in any form or by any means—graphic, electronic, or mechanical, including photocopying, recording, taping, Web distribution or information storage retrieval systems—without the written permission of the publisher.

Every effort has been made to trace the owners of copyrighted material.

Cover credit: © Chris Brackley/Fortean Picture Library

LIBRARY OF CONGRESS CATALOGING-IN-PUBLICATION DATA

Ghosts and Poltergeists / Terry O'Neill, book editor.
    p. cm. — (Fact or fiction?)
  Includes bibliographical references and index.
  ISBN 0-7377-1377-1 (pbk. : alk. paper) — ISBN 0-7377-1376-3 (lib. : alk. paper)
    1. Ghosts. 2. Poltergeists. I. O'Neill, Terry, 1944– . II. Fact or fiction? (Greenhaven Press)
  BF1461 .G494   2003
  133.1—dc21
                                                                    2002027153

Printed in the United States of America

133.1 Gho
1190 0415   4-16-03   LCL

Ghosts and Poltergeists
/
SDW

LeRoy Collins
Leon County Public Library
200 W. Park Avenue
Tallahassee, Fl. 32301

Contents

Foreword

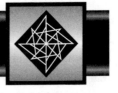

"There are more things in heaven and earth, Horatio, than are dreamt of in your philosophy."
—William Shakespeare, *Hamlet*

"Extraordinary claims require extraordinary evidence."
—Carl Sagan, *The Demon-Haunted World*

Almost every one of us has experienced something that we thought seemed mysterious and unexplainable. For example, have you ever known that someone was going to call you just before the phone rang? Or perhaps you have had a dream about something that later came true. Some people think these occurrences are signs of the paranormal. Others explain them as merely coincidence.

As the examples above show, mysteries of the paranormal ("beyond the normal") are common. For example, most towns have at least one place where inhabitants believe ghosts live. People report seeing strange lights in the sky that they believe are the spaceships of visitors from other planets. And scientists have been working for decades to discover the truth about sightings of mysterious creatures like Bigfoot and the Loch Ness monster.

There are also mysteries of magic and miracles. The two often share a connection. Many forms of magical belief are tied to religious belief. For example, many of the rituals and beliefs of the voodoo religion are viewed by outsiders as magical practices. These include such things as the alleged Haitian voodoo practice of turning people into zombies (the walking dead).

There are mysteries of history—events and places that have been recorded in history but that we still have questions about today. For example, was the great King Arthur a real king or merely a legend? How, exactly, were the pyramids built? Historians continue to seek the answers to these questions.

Then, of course, there are mysteries of science. One such mystery is how humanity began. Although most scientists agree that it was through the long, slow process of evolution, not all scientists agree that indisputable proof has been found.

Subjects like these are fascinating, in part because we do not know the whole truth about them. They are mysteries. And they are controversial—people hold very strong and opposing views about them.

How we go about sifting through information on such topics is the subject of every book in the Greenhaven Press series Fact or Fiction? Each anthology includes articles that present the main ideas favoring and challenging a given topic. The editor collects such material from a variety of sources, including scientific research, eyewitness accounts, and government reports. In addition, a final chapter gives readers tools to analyze the articles they read. With these tools, readers can sift through the information presented in the articles by applying the methods of hypothetical reasoning. Examining these topics in this way adds a unique aspect to the Fact or Fiction? series. Hypothetical reasoning can be applied to any topic to allow a reader to become more analytical about the material he or she encounters. While such reasoning may not solve the mystery of who is right or who is wrong, it can help the reader separate valid from invalid evidence relating to all topics and can be especially helpful in analyzing material where people disagree.

Introduction

Marlene Akhtar lived in an old house in Hot Springs, South Dakota. The twenty-room home was built as a guesthouse in 1891 in a town known for its gambling and carousing. One evening during the mid-1970s, Akhtar was sitting in her living room, relaxing. She looked up and saw across the room an elegant woman in a beige lace dress in a style from the previous century. The woman was walking down the staircase from the second floor. The woman's dark hair was pinned back in a bun, and she looked straight ahead, descending gracefully, her hand on the stair rail. As Akhtar watched, the woman disappeared. The lady in beige was only the first of several ghosts Akhtar saw during the eleven years she lived in the house, report Michael Norman and Beth Scott in *Haunted America*.

In downtown Sacramento, California, a group of ghost researchers recently investigated the rumored haunting of the Sacramento Theatre Company. Over the past half-century, many theater patrons and workers have reported seeing strange lights and forms with a pinkish aura. Using cameras and other tools, the researchers set up shop—and captured several baffling light patterns on their infrared film. Other investigators have recorded unexplained footsteps crossing one of the theater's stages.

Annemarie Schaberl was a young secretary in a law office in Rosenheim, Germany. In November 1967 strange things began happening in the office. Lightbulbs exploded, electrical fuses blew out, copy machine fluid spilled when no one was nearby, pictures fell off walls or rotated out of kilter, and the telephone system spontaneously dialed the local time number over and over, hundreds of times a day. When parapsychologist (a person who studies unexplained phenomena) Hans Bender investigated, he determined that the mysterious events were somehow connected to nineteen-year-old Schaberl, even though there was no evidence that she was deliberately doing anything to cause these things. Sure enough, when Schaberl left the job, things returned to normal.

The Belief in Ghosts and Poltergeists

People have been reporting incidents like the three described above since time began. For example, Pliny the Younger, an ancient Roman historian, reported during the first century A.D. about a house haunted by a thin old man wearing clanking chains. One night, the ghost led a guest in the home to a spot outside. The next day, men dug up the spot and found a pile of bones buried with rusty chains. When they gave the bones a proper burial, the ghost disappeared and was never seen again.

People in every country believe in ghosts. In the United States today, according to a recent national poll, 42 percent of the population—and 67 percent of widows—have reported contact with the dead. Most of these people say they saw an apparition (ghost), but half also heard one, one-fourth say they were touched by one, and one-fifth say they talked to one.[1] But not everyone believes in ghosts. And scientists note that no scientific evidence proves without question that ghosts exist. Yes, *something* is causing people to see ghostly images, *something* is causing the sounds of ghostly footsteps, *something* is flinging light bulbs and vases to the ground. But there is little agreement as to what is causing these mysterious events—and little agreement that it is the same cause each time.

Defining Ghosts and Poltergeists

Ghosts and poltergeists are not the same thing. Ghosts are usually associated with the dead, but poltergeists are associated with the living. People sometimes think the two are related because both can involve unexplained phenomena, sometimes very similar in nature. Here are some typical manifestations:

A	B
• A human or animal form appears, either solid or transparent; it appears and disappears without regard to the rules of physics.	• Objects fly about the room, electrical connections go on and off, furniture moves, stones fall from the sky, all with no apparent cause.
• Rappings, thumpings, and other noises have no discernible source.	• Rappings, thumpings, and other noises have no discernible source.
• Disembodied voices are heard.	• Disembodied voices are heard.
• A cold draft accompanies the apparition.	• A person's hair is pulled or skin is pinched by invisible fingers, or unexplained welts appear on the person's body.
• The apparition is usually seen in the same place by various witnesses; it may appear occasionally or frequently for many years.	• The puzzling activities usually occur in the presence of a particular person.

Although one cannot be too hard and fast with something as insubstantial as a ghost or a poltergeist, the items in column A are more characteristic of ghosts, and those in column B are more characteristic of poltergeists. Notice that some items appear in both columns, but some do not. Although both ghosts and poltergeists thump and knock, it would be unusual to *see* a poltergeist, and it would be unusual for a ghost to do something *physical* to witnesses, like pinch them or pull their hair.

A ghost is usually thought of as the spirit of a dead person. It can manifest, or make itself known, by appearing as a vision or through sounds or voices. Many times an odor accompanies a ghost. During the late-nineteenth-century parapsychologist Frederic W.H. Myers defined a ghost as *"a manifestation of persistent personal energy,* or as an indication that some kind of force is being exercised after death which is in some way connected with a person previously known on earth."[2]

Poltergeists are different. Poltergeists are a kind of energy or spiritual entity, but they are not the spirit of a dead person. As stated above, a poltergeist is usually associated with a living person, most often a preadolescent, a teenage girl, or an adult undergoing severe stress and repressing strong emotions. The case involving Annemarie Schaberl, described at the beginning of this introduction, is a classic poltergeist case. She is a classic focus person—the person around whom the poltergeist activities center. She was young, disliked her job, and was bored by the menial tasks she had to perform. The parapsychologist concluded that Schaberl was unconsciously focusing her mental energy to create the baffling chaos in the office.

Kinds of Ghosts

Some parapsychologists classify ghosts into several categories. G.N.M. Tyrrell, a well-known parapsychologist of the mid-twentieth century, identified these categories of apparitions—or the supernatural appearance of a person, animal, or other creature:

- Experimental cases: A living person tries to make his or her spirit visible to another person in another location.
- Crisis apparitions: A living person sees the spirit of someone recognizable who is undergoing a crisis, such as a life-threatening accident or even death.
- Postmortem apparition: The spirit of a deceased person is seen long after his or her death.
- Hauntings: A spirit habitually appears in a place.

Of these, the last three are typically considered ghosts. Other experts have made other classifications. For example, Hilary Evans and Patrick Huyghe, authors of *The Field Guide to Ghosts and Other Apparitions*, divide ghosts and apparitions into these groups:

"Ghosts of the past," including

- Time slip: An event from the past reenacted in spirit form; for example, some visitors to the Gettysburg Civil War battlefields have reported seeing an apparition of an entire battle reenacted, noises, horses, cannons, and all.
- Revenant: A postmortem ghost that appears only once or a few times.
- Haunter: A ghost that appears repeatedly over an extended period of time.

"Ghosts of the present," including

- Crisis apparition: A ghost that appears during a time of crisis; for example, a person may see a loved one's apparition at the moment of that loved one's death.
- Noncrisis apparition: When a person sees another living person's "ghost."

"Ghosts of the future," including

- Harbinger: A spirit that gives a warning.
- Time slip: A ghostly scene that previews the future.

In addition to all of the ghost types listed above, those who believe in spirits say there are other spiritual entities that are not ghosts—not the spirit of a dead (or a living) person. These include such things as demons and angels.

Contacting Ghosts

People have been trying to contact ghosts far longer than anyone has tried to study them scientifically. In many cultures, ghosts are viewed as intermediaries between this world and the world of the gods. In China, for instance, it is traditional to have an altar someplace in the house honoring the family's ancestors, who include any deceased family member, not just ancestors from many generations ago. The family gives food and other offerings to encourage the ancestors to intervene with the gods and bring the family good fortune.

In modern Western cultures, especially Great Britain and the United States, people may honor the memories of their deceased loved ones, but they do not typically view ghosts as intermediaries or entities with whom to communicate. In fact, in these cultures, ghosts have more often been considered the stuff of fiction—the famous ghost in Shakespeare's *Hamlet*, the creatures that haunt the stories of Edgar Allan Poe, and the phantoms depicted in movies like the comedy *Ghostbusters* and the horror film *Candyman*, for example. But during the nineteenth century an important period of spiritualism (or communication with spirits or ghosts) occurred, and this period has influenced the study of ghosts even to the present.

In the United States the "birth" of spiritualism is often credited to the Fox sisters. In 1848 fifteen-year-old Katie Fox and her twelve-year-old sister, Maggie, accidentally began communicating with a rapping spirit. The girls would ask a question, and the spirit would rap different signals for *yes*, *no*, and letters of the alphabet. The spirit rapped out that he was the ghost of a murdered peddler. The Foxes' neighbors soon heard of this wondrous phenomenon. When the Foxes' cellar was dug up, human bones were found. When the local press heard the story, they wrote about it, and soon the Fox sisters were famous. With their much older sister, Leah, as their manager, they began traveling around the country, holding séances in which they allegedly communicated with many different spirits.

The Fox sisters' success inspired a rash of other "mediums" (those who communicate with spirits) who contacted spirits at séances. The séances originally took place in private family homes, but soon they were conducted on large public stages. A séance usually took place in a darkened room (or auditorium). The medium would go into a trance state to contact the spirits, which might communicate through rappings, as happened with the Fox sisters' early performances. But the spirits also made their presence known by making a table float or by taking over the body of the medium. For instance, bereaved people could recognize the voice of their dead child or parent coming from the medium's mouth. Sometimes a spirit appeared in human form. Often it was the ghost of someone close to one of the séance participants, but sometimes famous people's ghosts appeared as well. Sometimes a séance included an "apport"—an object that appeared out of nowhere. Sometimes this was an object connected to a familiar spirit, such as a grandparent's watch, but sometimes it was an odd trumpet or some other spirit object. Sometimes the medium exuded ectoplasm, a tissuelike substance that oozed out of the medium's mouth or appeared from elsewhere and was supposedly the substance of ghosts.

As one might imagine, séances could be very impressive. In fact, a religion grew up around them. Séances and mediums in general began to lose their reputation when the

Foxes confessed to fraud in 1888. (They said the rappings that had sounded when they were teenagers were made when they secretly cracked their toe joints.) However, the Spiritualist Church still exists, and many people believe it is possible to contact the spirits of the dead.

Some people today use devices like Ouija boards to help them communicate with spirits. A Ouija board has *yes, no,* the letters of the alphabet, and the numbers 0 through 9 printed on it. Users use a pointing device, which they believe is directed by a spirit, to spell out messages on the board. Other people still use mediums to help contact the dead. Today, a medium is more likely to be called a psychic, a reader, or a channeler. A psychic or a reader will act much like an old-time medium, sitting with someone at a table and attempting to use mental (psychic) powers to contact a spirit. They will sometimes "read" items like crystal balls, Tarot (fortune-telling) cards, or tea leaves. A channeler, like an old-time medium, is taken over by the spirit. Channelers also claim to host spirits other than ghosts, such as a guiding spirit from another location in the universe or from another spiritual dimension.

If Ghosts Exist, Why Do They?

A belief in ghosts is, of course, tied to a belief in an afterlife. In some cultures, people are believed to have two ghosts—a good one and an evil one. A ghost might also be called the "life force," "spirit," or "soul." In general, those who believe in ghosts believe that living beings are made up of two distinct parts, one physical and one spiritual. After the physical part dies, the spiritual part lives on. This becomes the ghost. Most cultures believe that the ghost exists by itself only for a finite period of time—that period between the body's death and when the spirit joins with other spirits in an afterlife. This might be heaven, hell, a great spiritual consciousness, or something else, depending on the culture's beliefs. Some cultures believe in reincarnation: When the physical body dies, the spirit is reborn into another body. But it is not necessarily reborn immediately; sometimes the ghost exists alone before it enters another body. (As noted above, some people also believe the spirit—or ghost—can leave the living body on occasion. An example is Tyrrell's experimental apparition, mentioned earlier. This book will focus on the most common understanding of ghosts: spirits of the dead.)

Even though many cultures believe there is a time when the ghost is between death and the afterlife, only a relatively small number of ghosts are seen, and some of these appear over and over for many, many years. Why do some ghosts never appear, and why do some seem to be between existences for so long? Some ghost researchers believe that ghosts are bound to a place or to a person for a time, and then they may be released to go to the afterlife. They believe a ghost appears either to help the living or because they have unfinished business they must take care of before they are released. Here are a few of the reasons some experts say ghosts stick around:

- *To help.* These ghosts may want to comfort or reassure the bereaved person or provide some other kind of help by making their existence known. Once that person has been helped, the ghost may move on to the afterlife. As noted above, many widows believe they are visited by the ghost of their dead spouse. Some people believe that ghosts are always scary, but most often, the visit of a ghost to a departed loved one is comforting. The widow or other bereaved person gets the sense that their beloved is at peace. They stop worrying and feeling resentment against the dead person, and the ghost never appears again, presumably having moved on to the afterlife.

- *Guilt or fear.* These ghosts may have done something terrible in their lifetime and are afraid to move on, fearing they will exist forever in a hellish place.
- *Bound to a loved one or beloved place.* The spirit of the deceased person is so obsessed with a person or a place that they refuse to let go.
- *Bound by loved ones.* The people these ghosts left behind are so obsessed with the deceased person that the ghost simply cannot get away.
- *Violent, unexpected death.* These ghosts died so suddenly and in such a violent way that they are discombobulated. They are angry and confused and may not realize that they are dead, or perhaps they are determined to help solve the mystery of their deaths. (The ghost described by Pliny the Younger, described near the beginning of this chapter, fits into this category.)

Some ghost experts believe that these last four types of ghosts must be set free by the living. The living must convince the ghost that it is right for them to move on to the afterlife.

Another theory about ghosts suggests that they are a sort of leftover energy from a person or even a place. Many ghosts appear at places where dramatic and violent events occurred—murders, battles, and so on. The theory is that there was so much emotional energy at these events that some of it remains. Another thought is that an emotional or spiritual (psychic) energy is left behind by the people who inhabit a place. Under certain conditions, this energy manifests itself as a ghost.

If Ghosts Do Not Exist, How Do We Explain Ghostly Phenomena?

A great many people do not believe in ghosts, and few scientists believe that ghosts have been scientifically proven real. What, then, can account for the ghostly manifestations—

thumping and knocking, visible apparitions, disembodied voices, and so on? Here are some of the most prominent explanations for ghosts and poltergeists:

- *Fraud.* From the early mediums to the present ones, investigators have found many examples of ghostly fraud. Mediums often use the same tricks that stage magicians use to fool audiences into believing that something mystical has happened. Old-time mediums usually conducted their séances in darkened rooms, where it was easy to conceal devices that could tip tables, mirrors that could give the illusion of a ghost, and strings or cables that could lower apports onto the scene.

  At supposedly haunted houses, investigators have found many kinds of devices that project the illusion of a ghost. They also have often discovered that witnesses have lied about what they saw.

  The article by James Randi in chapter three details the ways he believes a famous poltergeist was faked.
- *Natural conditions.* "Hauntings" are sometimes caused by such things as underground water streams making gurgling noises, drafts blowing through cracks in windows or walls, subtle vibrations from the earth's movement, and lights from passing cars reflecting off mirrors and windows.
- *Hallucination.* A hallucination is a vision caused by a drug, an illness, or a susceptible mental condition, such as the groggy state experienced when one is just waking from sleep. Some researchers have even shown how groups of people can experience the same hallucination.
- *Misperception.* A misperception is a misunderstanding of what you perceive. For example, you might hear a knocking sound and think it must be a ghost, but it is really a flapping window shade in another room or a woodpecker outside. Sometimes your state of mind can

cause you to misperceive. For example, if you have been reading about ghosts, seeing or hearing something unexpected can make you think of ghosts and perhaps make you think you are seeing or hearing one.

Early Ghost Investigations

At about the same time that spiritualism was at its height, certain people began to study ghosts seriously. Clearly, there were many fraudulent mediums. However, many people believed that spiritualism was basically sound, that people could indeed communicate with spirits. The Society for Psychical Research (SPR), founded in London in 1882, was one of the earliest serious organizations to study ghosts. The organization wanted to bring science and religion together to validate paranormal phenomena such as ghosts and extrasensory perception. One way to do this was to root out the frauds and try to find some way of proving that the others were real. SPR members compiled a massive amount of data on ghost reports, including the types of manifestations (apparitions, noises, and so on), the circumstances of the incidents, and other details. This material is still cited by ghost researchers today.

In the United States, the American Society for Psychical Research was founded in 1885. By the early years of the twentieth century, it was beginning to establish scientific standards for studying ghosts.

Several famous people were involved in the early search for the truth about ghosts. Sir Arthur Conan Doyle, author of the Sherlock Holmes stories, is famous for popularizing the scientific method of detection. Yet he accepted spiritualism with little question. Harry Houdini, the famous stage magician, was a friend of Doyle. However, the two men were on opposite sides of the ghost question. Houdini desperately wanted to believe so that he could communicate with his beloved deceased mother, but he was never able to find any proof that such communication was possible.

During the 1930s Harry Price was probably the best-known "ghost buster." His most famous case involved Borley Rectory, a large brick house built in 1863. The house was said to be haunted by a phantom nun and other ghosts. Poltergeist events also occurred there. Price visited the home several times over several years, interviewing the people who lived there and thoroughly examining the premises. In 1937 he leased the house for a year and established a team of some forty people to aid in investigating the house. The group used movie and still cameras to prove whether objects moved by no visible means. The group also included mediums, who said they made contact with the dead nun. Price wrote a book titled *The Most Haunted House in England*. After Price's death, he was accused of fraud, and witnesses came forth to testify that Price had caused some of the ghostly phenomena himself.

"Ghost Busting" Today

Today, ghost busters typically take one of two approaches to investigating an alleged haunting. They take a psychic approach or a scientific-detection approach.

The psychic approach to ghost investigation involves mediums or psychics. The investigator or investigating team believe they can find a ghost, communicate with it, and, often, convince it to leave. The article in chapter one by Ed and Lorraine Warren provides a glimpse into how this is done. The psychic may walk through the haunted place or may concentrate on a particular area the ghost is thought to inhabit. Then it is a matter of using mental power to try to communicate with any ghostly inhabitant. Sometimes the psychic is successful (as Lorraine Warren said she was at West Point), but sometimes no communication is ever achieved.

Gertrude Schmeidler, a well-known parapsychologist, established a systematic psychic approach. She had floorplans made of the haunted site, then she interviewed witnesses about their experiences and had them mark places on the plans where they witnessed ghostly phenomena. She then gave a group of psychics unmarked floorplans and had them walk through the site, mark any places where they sensed something unusual, and describe what they sensed, both factually (a cold spot) and emotionally (anxiety). If the witnesses and the psychics marked the same places and sensed similar things, Schmeidler considered it significant evidence of a ghost.

The scientific-detection method usually involves a substantial amount of low- or high-tech equipment. Like a police detective, the investigator interviews witnesses and thoroughly examines the scene for clues. He or she also looks for any indication of possible natural causes for the phenomena, such as creaky floorboards or an underground stream. An investigating team may use a grid to break down the areas of the haunted place, examining each part of the grid separately and comparing the results to see if any anomalies (unexplained phenomena) exist. These investigators typically use some or all of the following: still cameras, movie or digital cameras, special film (such as infrared), tape recorders, thermometers, tri-field meters (these cut out electromagnetic energy generated by household appliances and pick up other such energy), Geiger counters, and thermal imaging detectors. The article in chapter one by Joshua P. Warren describes an investigation using such tools.

Ghost investigators hope, of course, to actually film or tape-record a ghost—or to discover a clear explanation for the phenomena that convinced witnesses they saw a ghost. But more often, if they are lucky, their film captures strange blobs of light and their tape recorder captures sounds that barely resemble words.

To date, ghost investigators have found plenty of evidence that convinces those who already believe in ghosts but not enough evidence to convince skeptics.

Notes

1. CNN/*USA Today*/Gallup poll, http://tristateghosts.homestead.com.
2. Quoted in Rosemary Ellen Guiley, *The Encyclopedia of Ghosts and Spirits*, 2nd ed. New York: Checkmark Books/Facts On File, 2000, p. 151.

Chapter 1

Fact or Fiction?

Ghosts Are Real

Houses Are Haunted by Those Who Lived There

Lance Morrow

One of the explanations that ghost researchers give for haunted places is that the house (or other site) retains the spiritual energy of the people who lived—or died—there and the events that occurred there, especially if the people underwent great emotional upheaval or the events were emotion charged. Sometimes, a witness experiences this spiritual energy as a vague feeling of uneasiness or perhaps as lights and sounds that have no known source. At other times, witnesses experience something much more dramatic. For example, many people have reported witnessing the ghostly reenactment of Civil War battles at Gettysburg. Lance Morrow, a regular columnist for *Time* magazine, discovered that his ability to perceive these leftover spiritual energies helped him when he was house hunting.

From "A Mystic of Houses," by Lance Morrow, *Time*, June 30, 1997. Copyright © 1997 by Time, Inc. Reprinted with permission.

I claim, half-seriously, to be a mystic of houses. When I walk into a house, I think I know—that is, I feel—the emotional history of the place. Everyone knows that a house has an aura, as a person does—an atmosphere, a vibration that is characteristic and unmistakable. I am abnormally sensitive to houses, as a dog is a genius about smells, or as a soldier who took a bullet a long time ago might be sensitive to changes in weather. I mention all this because a ghost has turned up.

My wife and I went house hunting in a rural county. The exercise sharpened my house-mystic's faculty. We inspected dozens of houses, led up and down dirt roads and blacktops by a real estate agent. He would recite the history of each house and, most discreetly, tell something about the owners ("The kids are grown; they're moving back to the city," or, once the agent knew us better, "They're getting a divorce—she's taken up with the contractor"). As I skimmed up gossip, my eyes would frisk the house in an abstracted way, taking in mood, angles of light and shadow, and after that, piecing together what I thought was the house's story.

Once we inspected a yellow brick farmhouse nestled in a fairy-tale little valley, its cow pastures enclosed by wooded ridges of old-growth maple, birch and hemlock. I wanted the house. Then I walked inside and knew I didn't want it anymore. I picked up . . . a kind of rage, a claustrophobia, a violence. The atmosphere of the house was red and gave off a low, unwholesome electricity, a Satan's hum. The ceilings pressed down. The walls seemed to be stained by anguish. I burst out of the house as if from a room full of poisoned gas.

A house's joy may announce itself as vividly as its misery, or an inherent contentment as readily as a permeating sorrow. The personality embedded there may be stolid, smug, hospitable, plainspoken, snobbish. I cannot explain the physics, but I imagine that the passions and attitudes and conversations, the laughs and screams of past occupants come, over a period of years, to saturate the walls and wallpapers and paints and floors and beams, as the sweats and oils of a man's head get into the band and felt of his hat. Something in our core detects house moods in the way a forming infant picks up the moods of its domicile, the womb. A house transmits different influences the way a pregnant mother does, depending on whether she gets drunk at night or listens to Mozart.

It is easy to detect an alcoholic house—it smells of its sorrows, smudged rages and dead brain cells. A house may be possessed more easily by a demon than a person may; a person has consciousness and mobility and a measure of will, all of which he may use to flee. A house is immobile, a cruder and more passive organism, though possessing a soul nonetheless, and is articulate in its own language. A house may be in a state of grace or in a state of mortal sin. If it harbors hatred or incest or violence or some other misery, the house will absorb the facts and become an archive of the unhappiness. The reverse is true. Love gives a house a radiance. All of us know these things.

The resonances of a new house may be premonitions rather than memories. One day at dusk in late November, I visited the freshly minted suburban house of a young woman, recently married. Her husband was at work. The woman did not work. She sat alone at home and waited for his return—a bride marooned in desolate, treeless suburbia. I visited the woman in the early '70s. I pieced together, from that half-hour, what proved to be an accurate scenario of the course that American feminism would follow. The house predicted everything.

My wife I and finally bought a 150-year-old white farmhouse on a dirt road. Everyone who visits speaks with wonder about the house's emanations. A family lived here happily for many years. The old man's wife died in her 70s; he lived on in the house and died at an advanced age. The house radiates an astonishing sweetness.

Several times in the past two weeks, my wife has wakened at 4 in the morning and heard footsteps in the house—a man's footsteps, she thinks, not stealthy, but matter-of-fact, like those of a man going about early-morning chores. I have listened, heard the sounds and gone to look, and concluded that the furnace has been making footstep noises.

I don't quite believe it. An amputee may harbor in his nerves the ghost of the missing leg—his former completeness. Perhaps out of habit, our house believes, down in its planks and nails, that the old man still gets up at 4 and busies himself at coffee and oatmeal. A puttergeist. I am happy to share the house with the ghost (though I sleep later than 4 in the morning and wish that at that hour he would keep it down). I trust my wife and I will eventually replace the old man's ghost in the house's affections.

Fire-Starting Poltergeists

Vincent H. Gaddis

If you were to suddenly find objects flying around your room and crashing to the floor, hear unexplained knockings and thumpings, and see your lights turn on and off, you might think you have a poltergeist. Poltergeists, or "mischievous spirits," do all of these things and more. Most of their activities are merely annoying, but sometimes they can become dangerous.

People often think of poltergeists as a type of ghost. But researchers do not consider them to be ghosts. A ghost is typically defined as the spirit of a departed living being. A poltergeist, on the other hand, is directly connected to a living "focus person." That is, poltergeists' activities generally seem to be directed toward a particular person or somehow revolve around that person. The focus person is typically troubled, such as a teenager going through difficult puberty or a person repressing a great deal of anger. Although some poltergeists are discovered to be hoaxes, others are not easily explained. Some researchers believe that poltergeist activities

Excerpted from *Mysterious Fires and Lights*, by Vincent H. Gaddis (Garberville, CA: Borderland Sciences Research Foundation, 1967). Copyright © 1967 by Vincent H. Gaddis. Reprinted by permission of the publisher.

are a form of psychokinesis—in other words, that the focus person is somehow, either consciously or unconsciously, causing the bizarre activities through mental power.

In the following selection, Vincent H. Gaddis describes a particular kind of poltergeist, one that starts fires. Gaddis was a newspaper reporter and author of many books and articles about the unexplained.

In *Time* magazine, April 7, 1947, appears a short, short story with a sad ending: "In Woodstock, Vt., a fire broke out in the basement of the Wendall Walker home on Sunday; the staircase caught fire on Monday; an upstairs partition blazed on Tuesday; the jittery Walkers moved out on Wednesday; the house burned down on Thursday."

Professional and trained volunteer firemen always attempt to make certain that a fire is totally extinguished on the first call, and if this requires some extra work with the axe and hose line, that's too bad. The image of a department is tarnished if its men have to return to the scene because an overlooked smoldering spark between the walls or under the roof has broken out in flames.

In the hundreds of fires I covered as a newspaper reporter and volunteer fireman myself, I can recall a number of instances when firemen had to respond to a second alarm, but very few when they had to return three or more times. In these latter cases, however, the fires were not in private homes, but in large warehouses and factory buildings containing highly combustible materials. The chief, recognizing the possibility of further outbreaks, almost always left an engine company at the scene.

The fires we are about to outline are in a different category. They obey certain physical and psychical laws we are only beginning to comprehend. Their origin is not only startling, but chilling. . . .

Mysterious Fires

The fantastic fires at the William Hackler farm home near Odon, Indiana, were reported by the Travelers Insurance Company in an advertisement in the former *Collier's* magazine for April 19, 1941. The house had never been wired for electricity, and there was no fire in the kitchen range during the period of the phenomenon.

The first fire broke out at 8 A.M. on the west side of the house near a second-floor window. Members of the Odon Fire Department extinguished it and left, but they had no sooner arrived back at their station when they received a second alarm. This time the fire was in a layer of paper between the springs and mattresses of a bed in a first-floor room. Then, between 8 and 11 A.M., nine fires broke out in different parts of the house, all without apparent cause.

"Some were so strange as to tax the belief of the most credulous persons who visited the place," the report states. "A calendar on a wall went up in a quick puff of smoke. Another fire started in a pair of overalls on a door. A bedspread was reduced to ashes while neighbors, standing in the room, stared in amazement. A book taken from a drawer of a desk was found to be burning inside, though the cover of the volume was in perfect condition."

By eleven o'clock that night, twenty-eight fires had broken out, and the weary Odon firefighters had requested help from the Elnora Fire Department. The Hacklers moved out and spent the night on beds set up under trees in the yard. The next week, the family abandoned the house, tore it down, and salvaged the lumber to build a new home.

Some of the explanations advanced were as weird as the fires themselves. It was suggested that the Hackler farm was in the center of a strong magnetic field saturated with static electricity. Another notion was that gases from an old well had permeated the structure, finally bursting into flame by spontaneous combustion.

"These and other solutions appear none too plausible," the report concluded. "The story remains even to fire officials a most baffling mystery.". . .

There was a fire on the second floor of the Douglas MacDonald home in Glace Bay, Nova Scotia, on the afternoon of April 16, 1963. Damage was extensive. Although the origin of the blaze was not known, it was suspected that an electrical short was the cause. The current was cut off, and the family, consisting of Mr. and Mrs. MacDonald and three adopted daughters, the youngest aged 21, moved to temporary quarters.

Two days later, Mrs. MacDonald was cleaning up debris when an insurance adjuster called. While they were talking, they smelled smoke. They found a new fire on the second floor, which they put out without difficulty. The adjuster left, and other members of the family arrived to help in the cleaning.

A few hours later another fire broke out on the second floor. It spread rapidly, and firemen were forced to fight the flames through the windows. The blaze not only caused additional damage to the house, but destroyed some new furniture that had been moved in to replace that lost in the first fire.

Although faulty wiring could not have caused any of the later fires, since the power was still off, the MacDonalds decided to have the house rewired. They remained living in another part of town while the work of restoration was in progress. On May 16, just one month after the original fire, Mrs. MacDonald and daughter Betty stopped by to see how the work was coming along.

As soon as they entered, they noticed smoke and called firemen. The smoke was traced to the first-floor bathroom. Inside an enclosed recess a pile of papers in a cardboard box was found ablaze. The firemen soaked the papers and left. By this time they should have known better and remained. They were back in less than half an hour.

The fire was in a bedroom closet and was burning fiercely. After it was extinguished, the irritated and perplexed firefighters tried unsuccessfully to find a cause. The two fires had occurred over ten feet apart on either side of a wall. There was no trace of fire, or even heat, between the two places within the flooring or along the basement ceiling. There was no sign of fire inside or outside the wall. It was obvious that both fires had originated where they were found, yet there were no materials at either place that could cause spontaneous combustion.

Foolishly, the firemen left. Two hours later they were back, putting out a blaze inside a wall cupboard. The fire had apparently started on the inner surface of the cupboard door, and the wall behind the cupboard was undamaged. The cupboard contained only the usual kitchen equipment. It did not contain any oily rags or suspicious chemicals. The firemen left.

It is unlikely that any pinochle game was completed that spring afternoon at the Glace Bay Fire Station. After each fire the boys have work to do. The primer tank must be refilled, hose lines laid out or hung to dry, equipment and boots cleaned. Nor do firemen enjoy riding over the same old route to the same old place, but duty comes before pleasure.

Half an hour later they were back at the MacDonald home. The fire, a small one this time, was on the back porch, and was quickly extinguished. The fire chief called the police chief. An officer was assigned to remain at the house.

Sympathetic, curious neighbors came to call. As they

were talking to Mrs. MacDonald and her daughter, one visitor suddenly shouted, "Look, there's another fire!" A section of wallboard was smoking. A neighbor pried it loose and stamped out the fire. The policeman examined the wallboard. There was no smoke or sign of fire in the space behind the wall. The bewildered officer ordered everyone out of the house.

This was the final outbreak. Investigators reached no conclusions. Insurance failed to cover all of the loss. Weeks later the family moved back into the house and as far as I know is still there.

In 1963, Mr. MacDonald, retired and living on a pension, was 69, his wife four years younger. Mrs. MacDonald was a former officer and lifelong active member of the Salvation Army. With no children of their own, they had, through the years, adopted and raised a number of sons and daughters. At the time of the fires three daughters remained in the home—Sheilah and Marie, both 25, and Betty, 21. In addition, the couple had at various times taken temporary care of children placed with them by a child welfare agency. Why were they plagued? . . .

Poltergeists

The preceding cases are examples of poltergeist fires. And what are poltergeists? The old German word means noisy or mischievous ghosts, and [in the 1940s] it was little known beyond the borders of psychical research. Today it's in the vocabulary of every well-informed newsman, although it is often, and quite incorrectly, used as a synonym for ghost or spirit.

Modern parapsychologists recognize that the poltergeist is not a disembodied spirit. It displays no knowledge of a previous earthly life or of a spirit realm. Its intelligence is subnormal and immature, and it exhibits little originality.

Usually it is harmless, but mischievous and destructive in a childish manner. Occasionally, however, it can be malicious and dangerous. It is intimately associated with a living person, not a place.

The living person or "agent" so involved is the unconscious creator of the poltergeist, and the cause of the phenomenon. Sometimes such agents are adults, but in the great majority of cases they are young persons of adolescent age who have subconscious mental traumas or frustrations. The awakening sexual powers and the bodily changes at such periods, are directly connected with the energies that produce the phenomena. Girls are the usual agents. The late Harry Price, founder of the University of London Council for Psychical Investigation who studied thousands of cases, estimated that there were nine girl agents for every boy.

Agents are often overworked maids or servant girls, neurotic adopted children or orphans, or emotionally disturbed sons and daughters. The poltergeist is a projected segment of the subconscious mind of such persons, giving vent aggressively to the trauma or repression. . . .

Of all psychic phenomena, the poltergeist is probably the oldest and most widespread. It is found in ancient literature, going back to the Egyptians. It has appeared in countries from the equator to the poles. It crops up in tropical jungles and world capitals. And at all times and in all cultures the pattern of its activity has been the same, with only minor variations.

Poltergeist disturbances, with a few exceptions, are short-lived simply because the conditions that make them possible are transitory. The most frequent type of phenomenon is psychokinesis—the movement and levitation of objects, showers of stones, the breaking of dishes and bottles. Next comes sounds, which may range from raps on the walls to apparent explosions that shake the windows. Outbreaks of fires, fortunately, are by no means as frequent.

There are rare fraudulent cases, of course. Children, as a rule, consciously work off their aggressions and may attempt to throw the blame on a "ghost," but such antics are easily detected. In poltergeist psychokinesis the objects are not thrown; they drift through the air, usually at a slow speed; they move in curves and may suddenly change direction. Often they are warm and even hot to the touch. There is, in these cases, a force that counters gravity.

There is no doubt about the paraphysical nature of these manifestations which have been observed by hundreds of reputable witnesses.

Nevertheless, there is a general prejudice against real mystery. Perhaps it is a fear of the unknown that makes most people demand explanations. Nothing must exist beyond our compact, known world that we can't classify and pigeonhole. And so, no matter how incredible the phenomena, no matter how impossible it would be for a person to produce this phenomena by trickery, we have "confessions."

Crude Trickery and False Confessions

The agent, not knowing consciously that he caused the phenomena, seems at times to have a sense of guilt, some slight awareness of responsibility. Such agents can be pressured into confessions despite the fact that the phenomena could not have been performed by normal means.

Irritated investigators and frantic parents occasionally use force to gain confessions. The history of these manifestations is dotted with examples of boys being whipped and little girls slapped. In an English case reported by Harry Price, a determined investigator was arrested for assault and battery on the agent.

Again, the agent may be told either to reproduce the phenomenon supernormally or confess it was fraudulent. Out of vanity, some may then resort to crude trickery only to be caught. Others may simply make a false confession. In witchcraft days hundreds of persons, including "hysterical girls," confessed that they had sold their souls to the devil and had flown through the air to his "sabbaths" without undergoing torture. And these confessions were made with the knowledge that painful deaths would have to be faced.

False confessions occur much more commonly than many persons outside the field of psychology realize, according to Dr. Ian Stevenson, chairman of the Department of Neurology and Psychiatry at the University of Virginia School of Medicine. "A vague impression of guilt about something often suffices to motivate a false confession," he says. "Innocent persons have frequently confessed to serious crimes like murder, sometimes implicating innocent persons as accomplices. . . ."

Confessions, therefore, are simply worthless unless they also include an explanation of the *modus operandi* that is reasonable, practical, and fits the known facts. . . .

The Charles Willey Farm Fires

No story of strange fires ever received more publicity than the outbreak at Macomb, Illinois, during August 1948. Every daily newspaper in the United States and the leading journals of Europe carried the day-by-day reports, most of them on their front pages. Although I was unable to personally investigate the case (I was news editor of an Indiana radio station at the time), I talked with reporters who had been at the scene, in addition to collecting all wire service accounts.

The fires began at the Charles Willey farm, twelve miles south of Macomb, on August 7. The family consisted of Willey and his wife, aged in their sixties; Willey's brother-in-law, Arthur McNeil; and McNeil's two children, Arthur, Jr., 8, and Wanet, 13. McNeil was divorced and had custody of the children. His former wife was living in Bloomington, Illinois.

Small brown spots began appearing on the wallpaper in the five-room cottage. They were roughly two-to-three inches in diameter and were obviously from scorching. When the heat reached about 450 degrees Fahrenheit, it ignited the paper which burst into flames, but the source of this heat was a mystery. Day after day more spots and fires appeared. Neighbors came to help keep watch and fight the fires. Pans and buckets of water were placed in strategic locations throughout the house, and when a spot appeared it was drenched with water.

Macomb Fire Chief Fred Wilson was called in. He had Willey strip off the wallpaper, but then the brown spots that became fires appeared on the bare boards, in the wood plaster laths and even on the ceiling.

"The whole thing is so screwy and fantastic that I'm almost ashamed to talk about it," INS quoted Chief Wilson as stating. "Yet we have the word of at least a dozen reputable witnesses that they saw mysterious brown spots smoulder suddenly on the walls and ceilings of the home and then burst into flames."

During the week following August 7, fiery spots also appeared outside the house on the porch. Several curtains were ignited, a cloth lying on a bed was found in ashes, and an ironing board on the porch was burned. The National Fire Underwriters Laboratory reported that the wallpaper was coated with flour paste and was free of any roach repellent that might have contained a phosphorous compound.

In addition to insurance investigators, John Burgard, state deputy fire marshal, came to the farm. "Nobody has ever heard anything like this," UP quoted Burgard, "but I saw it with my own eyes."

During this week, approximately two hundred fires broke out, an average of almost twenty-nine a day. On Saturday, August 14, the blazes finally raged out of control and destroyed the cottage. Willey drove posts into the ground and with a tarpaulin made a makeshift tent. The McNeils moved into a garage. The next day—Sunday—while the Willeys were milking cows in the barnyard, the barn went up in flames. . . .

On Tuesday several fires broke out on the walls of the milkhouse, which was being used as a dining room. Thursday morning there were two more blazes. A stack of newspapers in a box was found burning in the chicken house. Minutes later Mrs. Willey opened a cupboard door in the milkhouse and discovered other newspapers smouldering on a shelf. Then, about 6 P.M. that day, the farm's second barn burned down in twenty-five minutes. A fire extinguisher salesman was at the scene with his equipment, but he was helpless. "It was the most intense heat I've ever seen," he told newsmen. Only six small outhouses now remained on the farm.

The Air Force Investigates

The following day as the Willeys and McNeils fled to a neighbor's vacant farmhouse a mile away, the United States Air Force flew into the mystery. Lewis C. Gust, chief technician at Wright Field, Dayton, Ohio, sent an expert to the farm to test for "very high frequencies and short waves." He thought the fires might be related to several unsolved airplane fires in which radioactivity was suspected of playing a part. "We can't afford to take any chances," he continued. "We must test anything, even if it sounds a bit farfetched."

In an interview with the *Chicago Sun-Times*, Gust said: "Suppose you had material that could be ignited by radio and you wanted to test it for sabotage value. Wouldn't you pick some out-of-the-way place like the Willey farm to make the test?"

Gust said scientists believed that powerful high frequency

or extremely short radio waves could touch off fires. For example, radar waves set off photographic flash bulbs in planes in flight. An unidentified Chicago scientist agreed that radioactivity or radio waves might cause "such disturbances," but added that it was—"highly unlikely because there had been no other reaction in the area."

By this time the farm was swarming with official and self-appointed investigators, reporters, and hundreds of curious spectators. It was estimated that a thousand sightseers visited the farm on Sunday, August 22. And with all the suggested explanations—ranging from fly spray, to radio waves, to gas in the ground—being disproved, the officials turned to the possibility of arson.

Two investigators did note a difference between the fires in the cottage and the later blazes. Professor John J. Ahern, of the Illinois Institute of Technology, suggested that combustible gases inside the walls might have caused the house fires, while those fires that destroyed the barns "sprang from different causes." State Fire Marshal John Craig said the burning of the house "looked like an accident," while the barn fires may have been "touched off by an arsonist."

A Teenage Fire-Starter?

At any rate, the mystery simply had to be solved, and on August 30 the solution was announced. The alleged arsonist was Wanet, Willey's 13-year-old niece, a slight red-haired girl. With incredible persistence, an unlimited supply of matches, and blessed with exceptionally nearsighted relatives and neighbors, she had started all the fires with matches!

According to Deputy Marshal Burgard, there had been a minor fire at the farmhouse where the family had moved. He had placed a box of matches in a certain position, and the box had been moved. Wanet was nearby, but at no time had the girl been observed holding a match. So he and

State's Attorney Keith Scott had taken little Wanet aside and, after "an hour's intensive questioning," she had confessed.

Wanet was unhappy. She didn't like living on the farm. She wanted to live with her mother in Bloomington. She didn't get any pretty clothes living with her father. Taken to Chicago for examination at the Illinois Juvenile Hospital, Wanet was found to be normal mentally by Dr. Sophie Schroeder, a psychiatrist. "She's a nice little kid caught in the middle of a broken home," the doctor said. Forgotten were the witnesses who had watched brown spots appear, spread, and burst into flames.

Forgotten were the fires on the ceilings. I haven't bothered to try it, but I'm certain I could flip matches at ceilings all day with perfect safety. Some of the reporters took Burgard's explanation with a heavy coating of salt. From Peoria, the nearest large city to Macomb, Gomer Bath, well-known columnist on the *Star*, probably covered the case with more care than any other newsman. He frankly didn't believe the girl's "confession."

But in the end everyone was more or less satisfied. Wanet was turned over to the custody of her grandmother. The insurance company paid Willey $1,800 for the loss of his home and two barns, and the farmer said he planned to rebuild his house. The reporters were able to wind up their stories and move on to new ones. And the reading public had a simple, acceptable solution.

We Have Encountered Ghosts

Ed and Lorraine Warren

Ed Warren and his wife, Lorraine, have been investigating ghosts and other entities since the 1940s. They were already well-known as investigators and banishers of ghosts, demons, and poltergeists when they were called in to investigate a house in Amityville, New York, that was said to be haunted by the spirits of a murdered family. The story of that haunting became a famous movie, *The Amityville Horror*.

Some ghost hunters use various kinds of instruments to detect a ghostly presence. The Warrens, however, rely on psychic communication. They claim that Lorraine is able not only to sense a ghost but to communicate with it and, often, banish it. She does this by encouraging it to "go to the light" that represents the afterlife.

The Warrens have published nine books about their investigations, and they founded the New England Society for Psychical Research, which investigates paranormal occurrences around the world. The following selection describes

Excerpted from *Ghost Hunters: True Stories from the World's Most Famous Demonologists*, by Ed and Lorraine Warren with Robert David Chase (New York: St. Martin's Press, 1989). Copyright © 1989 by Ed Warren, Lorraine Warren, and Robert David Chase. Reprinted by permission of the publisher.

their experience with ghosts when they visited the West Point military academy to give a lecture.

Set on part of a 16,000-acre military reservation and situated on the bank of the Hudson River in New York, West Point gives the impression of being a vast fortress of stone, brick, and mortar isolated from all civilization. In fact, the academy is only fifty miles from New York City.

The new visitor to The Point is first drawn to Washington Hall, a huge building in front of which sprawls the main parade ground.

As the limousine drove onto the grounds that day, Lorraine was overwhelmed by a sense of history. American flags snapped in the soft breeze; cadets in perfect formation marched by. Taking Ed's hand, she knew he felt the same way.

The first part of the Warrens' visit was given over to a tour led by Major Dean Dowling. The Warrens got to see firsthand how West Point had evolved—from a few buildings to the gigantic complex of the present.

Throughout the tour, Major Dowling, another example of West Point bearing, asked the Warrens many questions about their work. He seemed particularly interested in their work with ghosts.

Troubled Spirits

They soon were to learn why.

When they had finished the tour, Major Dowling asked the Warrens if they would accompany him to superintendent George Nolton's residence. At The Point, the superintendent is always an army lieutenant general who is in charge of the entire 16,000 acres, the military post, and the academy.

Nolton's residence was the Colonel Sylvanus Thayer home

(Thayer had been the West Point superintendent from 1817 to 1833). A Federal-style house of white-painted brick, at first it looked appealing to Lorraine.

But as she drew close—and even before Major Dowling began to talk about the problems associated with the house—Lorraine began to tremble slightly and hear the distant but unmistakable keening of troubled spirits, a keening that often rings in the ears of gifted psychics.

Major Dowling was forthcoming. As they entered the house, he told them of many strange incidents that had taken place there over the past year. Many eyewitnesses had seen a bed stripped down by invisible hands. After being made again, an unseen force would once more strip it a few minutes later. For this reason alone, certain people at the academy made a point of avoiding the Thayer house, however urgent their business with General Nolton.

But there were even more troubling problems.

During their many years of investigating the occult and the supernatural, the Warrens had often encountered examples of "apports" [objects that mysteriously disappear from one place and reappear in another location]. In most cases, apports are objects that prove the presence of supernatural beings.

Major Dowling showed the Warrens a bread board. In the center of the wooden board was a wet spot approximately the size of a slice of bread. No matter how often the board was dried—nor no matter what method was used for drying it—the wet spot remained. And had remained for many months.

Upon seeing the bread board, Lorraine knew for sure that the sensations she was feeling—slight chills, the distant keening sound, the strange play of light and shadow in corners of the house—indicated that they were in the presence of supernatural entities. For proof positive of this, Major Dowling told them of apparitions seen not only by General

Nolton and his wife but by overnight guests as well.

The litany of proof was familiar to Lorraine and Ed. Ghosts had demonstrated their presence not only by showing themselves but by knocking on walls and slamming doors and—perhaps most embarrassing—going through the personal belongings of guests. Everything from wallets and jewelry had been lifted and set down in some other part of the house. Clothes were torn from hangers and ripped from drawers.

There could be no doubt.

General Nolton's residence had been infested by ghosts. Their exact nature and purpose had yet to be determined.

Making Contact

An hour later Lorraine began to move through the house, room by room, and attempted to make contact with the ghosts that the general and his friends had seen. While not every attempt to contact the realm of the spirits is successful, Lorraine felt confident that with her background she could find out what was going on.

Her optimism, however, was soon quelled; the first three rooms yielded nothing—no response whatsoever from the spirits. She came to suspect that Major Dowling might doubt her special talents.

The process was the same in each room. Lorraine stood in the center of the room and "listened" through various means for any evidence of psychic activity. None.

In the fourth room, a surprise awaited her. She sat down in a lovely rocking chair and closed her eyes. Immediately she began experiencing the increased heartbeat and aural sensations that often accompany contact with ghosts.

Inexplicably, she began to feel a pressure on her arm, as if someone were gently prodding her. She knew now that there was definitely a supernatural presence in this room, but what she saw was so startling she was almost reluctant to reveal it.

To one of the major's aides, she said, "Would you happen to know if President Kennedy was ever in this room?"

The aide looked surprised. "Why, yes," he said. "This was the room he stayed in when he came to The Point."

Now Lorraine knew her emanation had been a valid one. She had not only sensed but glimpsed the image of President Kennedy, standing next to her, touching her gently on the shoulder so she would look up and see him. Long an admirer of the slain President, Lorraine felt an overwhelming sorrow during her last moments in the chair, the same rocker that John Fitzgerald Kennedy, with his well-known back problem, had also sat in.

After leaving the room where Kennedy had slept, Lorraine felt she might have solved the identity of the West Point ghost. But as she walked down the wide, sun-splashed hallway, she felt new emanations, far more troubling than the ones that had accompanied President Kennedy's image.

No, there were other ghosts in this venerable house. Her job was not done.

Two Angry Spirits

"The moment I walked into the master bedroom," Lorraine Warren revealed later, "I knew that this house was being troubled by a female presence. At the time, that was all I knew, but after half an hour in the room, I realized a lot more."

With Lorraine and Ed, plus Major Dowling and his aide, crowded into the master bedroom, the investigation centered on various china pieces and statues in the room, many dating from the Revolutionary War period.

"As I touched the pieces, I began to get a confusing signal," Lorraine explained. "The china that dated back two hundred years gave me no specific emanations at all—but there was new china and statuary that painted for me a picture of a very domineering, strong-willed woman.

"I left the room for a time and began walking around the rest of the house. The image of the domineering woman stayed with me, and I came to realize that it was she who troubled the air here—she who had unmade the beds and tossed personal belongings around in the guest rooms."

In a small, ancillary room, Lorraine stood for a time while the woman's presence filled the doorway. "I knew that the woman was a jealous, possessive spirit who felt the house belonged to her and who resented anybody else who lived here. This was not a dangerous spirit, but it was a troublesome one.

"I went back to the room I'd been in and told the major's aide what I'd discovered. 'Many pieces of china here belonged to a very strong-willed woman. Is that correct?'"

Startled, the aide revealed that between marriages, General Douglas MacArthur's wife had lived here. An insecure and somewhat angry woman, she took her supreme task to be running Thayer's house as it had never been run before. Servants feared her; even officers wilted before her stern presence.

The presence of a second spirit was thus explained . . . as was some of the more troubling behavior that had gone on in this house over the past year.

Still, as Lorraine walked around, she became aware of another presence—this one the true source of the icy chills she'd felt from time to time during the day.

JFK had been a most friendly spirit; Mrs. MacArthur, while meddlesome, was also essentially benign, given over to pranks but nothing more dangerous.

But something else was in the air . . .

Lorraine sensed . . . violence.

She continued to move around the house, taking time in

each room to touch furnishings and aged woodwork polished to a fine shine.

The sense of . . . violence . . . did not leave her.

Something terrible had happened here—

And somebody who had been involved in the violence still roamed the hall, still hid in the dusky shadows of each chill room.

But, having nothing more specific to go on than her intuition, Lorraine relented and accompanied the rest of the group to the dining hall, where they would have a feast the finest restaurant would be proud to serve.

After that, Ed and Lorraine spent a long evening addressing the West Point audience, officers and spouses as well as cadets.

The Warrens found the group not only fascinated with their talk and their slides that showed proof of various types of supernatural activity; they also were more than willing to take such phenomena seriously.

Banishing a Tyrant and Conversing with a Troubled Ghost

At the end of the evening, several officers and their wives asked the Warrens if they would be willing to return to Thayer house and try to contact the spirits Lorraine had described.

Puzzled and dismayed by the angry presence she had sensed in the house, Lorraine was only too willing to agree.

In the master bedroom, the men and women sat on the floor in a semicircle around the bed. The officers opened the collars of their uniforms as Lorraine closed her eyes and began the difficult and occasionally frightening process of contacting earth's other realm.

Almost immediately, Lorraine felt great energy surge through the room, a certain sign that a spirit was present.

She knew at once that Mrs. MacArthur was here. Lorraine, who happened to be sitting on the edge of the bed that Mrs. MacArthur had slept in, began to see the woman clearly. Everything she had assumed that afternoon about the woman—that here was a great, insecure tyrant of a woman whose presence was meant to challenge Lorraine's right to be there—was confirmed.

But Lorraine's strong will soon enough banished Mrs. MacArthur, and for the next half hour, the people from The Point and the Warrens enjoyed a pleasant discussion of the supernatural.

According to Ed, "It was really exciting, watching the future leaders of our country sitting there on the floor, dressed in their military garb, asking questions of us. There was no embarrassment whatsoever. Some of them had known, along with Lorraine and me, when Mrs. MacArthur's presence had come into the room. They had many more questions then about how to contact the other realm themselves."

The evening concluded with some of the guests getting the Warrens' address so they could get further information on the subject of the supernatural. Lorraine had never felt better about the skills she and Ed had shared for so many years.

But just as the Warrens were to leave—the limousine being readied in a nearby garage—Lorraine looked out the window and saw on the moon-silvered parade grounds a genuine apparition:

—a black man dressed in a turn-of-the-century uniform without braids or insignia of any kind (as if all privilege had been stripped away from him) standing sadly looking up at Thayer house.

This was the angry presence Lorraine had known about instinctively all day long.

Who are you?

(Still gazing up at her.) My name is Greer.

You are troubled.

(He helped her form an image in her mind: a small, cell-like room, where he seemed to be confined.) I am not free.

What happened to you?

(An overwhelming sense of sorrow. Greer, in his stripped-bare uniform, raised his sad eyes to Lorraine's and then vanished.)

Greer (she wanted to say), Greer—I can help you.

But he was gone, gone.

As the Warrens waited for their limousine in the soft smoky warmth of the autumn evening, Lorraine told one of the aides about Greer. She described the uniform but the aide shook his head. "There weren't any black people at The Point at that time."

Troubled, Lorraine and Ed went home. . . .

A Ghost Is Explained

A week later the aide Lorraine had shared her Greer story with called to say that he'd done some research and that there had, in fact, been a black man at The Point during the era Lorraine described. His name was indeed Greer, and he had killed another man there. Although guilty of the murder, Greer was cleared by a military court and exonerated.

As soon as the aide revealed this, Lorraine recognized Greer for what he was—an angry, sad spirit who could not accept his own guilt and therefore roamed The Point scaring people without really meaning to. People sensed his rage—most likely rage with himself for what he'd done—and were frightened by it.

Thus the troubled spirit had been identified and explained. The people at West Point were grateful for what the Warrens had done.

Ghosts Comfort the Living

Louis E. LaGrand

Thousands of people all over the world have reported seeing a loved one after his or her death. G.N.M. Tyrell, a researcher who studied ghosts and other paranormal phenomena, divided such sightings into three basic types: the crisis apparition, when the deceased is seen at his or her moment of death or shortly after; the postmortem apparition, which occurs twelve or more hours after the person's death; and hauntings, or continual apparitions, which are seen many times over a long period. Even people who do not believe in ghosts have reported such sightings. Are they real, or are they figments of people's imaginations? If they are real, why do they happen?

Louis E. LaGrand, the author of the following selection, believes the apparitions are real and that they serve more than one purpose: Not only do they prove that there is life after death, but they purposely bring a sense of comfort to the bereaved. LaGrand is a grief counselor, professor emeri-

Excerpted from *After Death Communication: Final Farewells*, by Louis E. LaGrand (St. Paul, MN: Llewellyn Press, 1997). Copyright © 1997 by Louis E. LaGrand. Reprinted with permission.

tus at the State University of New York, and the author of several books.

Adults and children of all ages have had contact experiences with deceased loved ones involving the actual presence of that person, usually in what they interpret as normal bodily form. In some cases, the deceased appears in two- or three-dimensional form. In others, the upper body or the face is seen, sometimes surrounded by a white light. With rare exceptions, . . . the deceased looks whole and in good health. Of course, of all types of extraordinary experiences which may occur when a person is mourning, the visual or postmortem experience is usually cause for judging the mourner as unstable or in need of professional care. The reason for this judgment is that we are talking about ghosts, visions, and apparitions, which conjure up all sorts of suspicions, fears, and apprehensions. These unfortunate dynamics are something that is part of our cultural heritage.

Visions of deceased loved ones (or for that matter, those who are still living) are judged abnormal by today's standards. However, as history constantly reminds us, visions have been an integral part of the development of civilizations and the bedrock of many religious organizations, not to mention their role in the dramas of discovery and invention. Still, there is a special stigma attached to seeing things that cannot be held in one's grasp or ordered up for visual inspection again and again. In fact, many visions are denied by those who experience them out of fear that they may indicate mental deterioration or insanity. And those who have them will tell you that it is not easy to find someone who will openly listen when they wish to talk about them. . . .

Although apparitions of the deceased may occur many years later, the most common vision or apparition which I have found appears to take place within the time frame of three or four weeks to several months after the death of the person. The place of appearance is usually in the familiar surroundings of the home. . . . Here are three examples. In the first, a college student I'll call Tina sees her father in the hallway of her home.

"He Didn't Look Like He Did Before He Died"

The funeral was finally over. It had been a long day. That evening I took a shower to try to relax. I got dressed and came out of the bathroom to make a warm drink in the kitchen. As I turned to the right I saw my father standing at the end of my hall. He had had several strokes before he died and was partially paralyzed. He didn't look like he did before he died. He was vibrant and healthy and looked the way be did before he was ever sick. He stood there a few seconds, smiled, and gently faded away. I think he wanted me to know he was going to heaven and that his pain was finally over. This experience helped me because I knew he was finally happy and not suffering anymore.

Tina, who had just turned twenty, was not at all surprised by her father's appearance. She had been very close to him and was glad to see him so healthy, since his long illness had dimmed her memory of how active he used to be.

The second example comes from the oldest subject I have interviewed about a contact experience, eighty-two-year-old Doreen. I spoke with her in the room in which she saw her husband about seven months after his sudden death. Doreen was alert, decisive, and, I must admit, a bit defensive. I mention that because as she ushered me in and we sat down, before I could ask a single question, she started with, "I want to tell you I never believed in this sort of thing." Here is her account of Ted's visit to her.

"He Was Always Caring"

I knew Ted since I was nine years old. We were childhood friends and I later learned, when I was sixteen, after our first date, he told one of his friends that someday he was going to marry me. We finally did get married in 1935—fifty-seven years of marriage. We had a good life and a great relationship. He was a salesman, humorous, and the type who could keep the party going. But as he got older he developed asthma and once when he went into the hospital for some routine tests, the doctor discovered that he had gallstones and had to have an operation.

I figured everybody can have a gall bladder operation. Well he had it, and it was successful, but he developed an infection and they had to go back in again a second time. The reason for the second operation was they couldn't control the infection (He had been in intensive care for three weeks). I should have known it was more serious, but the doctor and the nurse didn't think it was real serious either. At least that's the impression they gave me.

I used to go in every day and stay from 10:00 A.M. until 4:00 P.M. One day, I had just arrived home and they called and said to come right back because he was having trouble breathing. He died before I could get back because he couldn't get enough air. The last thing he had said to me before I had left two hours earlier was "You've been so good to me and for me." I don't know if he had a premonition that his time had come or not, but I didn't expect his death.

The day I had the apparition, I was sitting right in this chair reading the paper. It was about 4 o'clock in the afternoon. For some reason, I glanced over the top of the paper and saw Ted floating in a vertical position right across the doorway between this room and the kitchen. He was about three feet off the ground. I saw him from the knees up, his feet couldn't have been touching the floor. It didn't take long for it to happen but I sort of sat there in shock. Normally, I would have poo-pooed all of this but I definitely did see it. He was dressed and looked good. There wasn't much color to it all; he was sort of like in a vapor. I could understand it if it happened right away after his death because it's all on your mind. This was several months later.

I think he's still checking on me and making sure everything is okay. He was always caring, watching to see that everything goes right. You know, things have worked out very nicely. I always say my prayers each night. He's there and God is there with me. I am content with my life. . . .

In this third example of a postmortem vision, a grieving sister, who I will call Allie, not only sees her deceased brother, but is given encouragement by him.

"Allie, Everything Is All Right"

My brothers had always watched over me and I really had become too dependent on them for some of the things I should have been doing for myself. My brother Phil had been killed in the automobile accident which also involved my oldest brother who was seriously injured but survived. I was very close to Phil and could not accept what had happened. I was beside myself with grief. One evening, several days after his death I just passed out from all the stress and trauma. When I opened my eyes Phil was standing over me and said, "Allie, everything is all right."

Because it was so hard for our family to accept his death I believe he wanted everyone to know he was now at peace, he was OK. But he came to me when I was in special need.

In each of these incidents, survivors interpreted the experience to mean that they should go on with their lives. Significantly, Allie's vision occurs after having passed out. She could not have been seeking his appearance in her temporary blackout. The implication was that Phil knew the difficulty his family was having accepting his death, and was there to ease the burden. . . . In a similar way, Doreen was completely surprised with Ted's visit. She had been out for most of the day, came home, and decided to read the newspaper. Her grief work, according to her own evaluation, was going well. She had accepted Ted's death and was not thinking about him at the time he appeared. But his appearance convinced her that he was still concerned and wanted her to know. This was comforting for her.

Despite their importance, not all visions of the deceased are accepted by survivors. Sometimes survivors are scared by the appearance and fear they may be losing their sanity. This is what happened to Laura (not her real name) several years ago. I learned of it after speaking to a group of professional caregivers at a college on the topic of grief support. My speech included some information on how to deal with someone who experiences the extraordinary. It never fails that after introducing the topic of the unusual experiences of the bereaved as a normal part of the grief process, someone will approach me or send me a note regarding a personal experience. In this instance, a middle-aged woman waited until most of the other participants had left the room and came up to me with great anxiety in her eyes. Here is the account of her experience as she shared it with me with much feeling.

"I Thought I Was Losing My Mind"

My father committed suicide. We were all so upset, destroyed. We couldn't understand what would drive him to do such a thing. About three days later, I went over to his house to organize his possessions and take care of his clothing. As I was walking up the driveway to the house, I looked up at the large glass-enclosed front porch—and he was standing there as big as life. I was scared. I thought I was losing my mind. He was there for only a short period of time and when I looked again, he was gone. It was a chilling experience and has caused me lots of problems. What do you think of this?

This woman (who was an acquaintance of mine, though

not one I expected to share her inner fears with me) was very concerned that there was something wrong with her mind. She was in desperate need to hear that what had occurred was not at all an indicator of a mental disorder; that it happens to many people, that her father's presence could very well have been his attempt to ease her suffering. Normalizing the experience was a significant step for her.

Sometimes the deceased will be seen in a favorite reclining chair or at the table, even sitting at the foot of the bed. According to Carl Sandburg, Mary Todd Lincoln told her White House nurse after the death of little Willie that the child ". . .comes every night and stands at the foot of my bed, with the same sweet adorable smile he always had." Her visions ended after a short period of time, having fulfilled an important function. It is also common that the deceased looks healthy or indicates that he or she is whole again. This is what happened to Beverly, whose husband had died of a heart attack after having severe angina pains for several years. "I knew my husband was always in a lot of pain and would try to hide it from me," she said. "One evening, when I was home alone, he was suddenly there with me in the living room. He looked so good and alive. He stretched out his hands and said, 'See I have no more pain.' I was so relieved and for a moment happy because he was happy."

In many visual experiences, the person is seen in vivid detail, which includes clothing, gestures, and facial expressions. He or she arrives suddenly and is gone just as suddenly. Occasionally there is a reappearance, as happened with Darlene. Her father had died unexpectedly from a heart attack. He had left the house to go fishing and was later found on the beach with his fishing tackle at his side. It was 2:00 A.M. when a detective knocked on Darlene's door to inform her of his death. The succession of appearances of her father began shortly after his funeral and continued for several weeks. Here is her account.

"I Didn't Know What to Believe"

I would wake up to the doorbell ringing at 2:00 A.M. The first time it happened I thought that someone else had died. I put on my bathrobe and went downstairs to answer the door. As I opened the door and peeked out there stood my father. He was dressed in his red checkered shirt and his fishing hat just as he was on the last day when they found him on the beach. He wore that smile I always loved. But as soon as I opened the door all the way, he was gone. This went on for several weeks; it would be 2:00 A.M. I would hear the doorbell, put on my robe, go down and open the door, and he would be there smiling and then vanish. I didn't know what to believe, although it didn't really alarm me. Finally, I talked to a friend at my church who had a similar thing happen to her. She helped me a lot. A short time later it stopped.

Darlene accepted the series of appearances of her father, but told me she was perplexed at why they occurred, since the same repetitive pattern was followed each time. She wondered, after his third or fourth appearance, if there "was something I was doing to cause them or if I perhaps was fantasizing." It was fortunate that she was able to find someone at her church to talk with who had a very similar experience with the death of a loved one. Because Darlene was a professional caregiver, her questioning of the experience was thorough and ongoing.

Proof or Fantasy?

Darlene was in good company. None other than [psychologist] Carl Jung, who was very interested in the extraordinary and believed that by way of the collective unconscious we all share a common bond with those who have gone before us, questioned the one-time appearance of his deceased friend. In his autobiography *Memories, Dreams, Reflections*, he writes about his postmortem apparition and his hesitancy in accepting what was happening to him.

Jung had been lying awake one evening reviewing the events of the previous day which were dominated by the funeral of a friend who had died unexpectedly. He had been deeply moved and saddened by the death. Without warning, he suddenly sensed the presence of his friend standing at the foot of his bed. At the same time, Jung felt that his friend had made a gesture to follow him out of the bedroom. The inner visual images were at first considered nothing more than mere fantasy. But he toiled with the problem that if it was not a fantasy and it really was his friend standing there, he would be showing great disrespect by not responding to him. In either case, he had no proof. So he gave his friend the benefit of the doubt and reacted as though the event were real.

In his imagination, he followed his friend as he walked out of the bedroom, up the road to his friend's house, and into his study. Very methodically, he watched as his friend climbed on to a stool and showed Jung the second of five books with red bindings lying on the second shelf from the top. At that point the vision ended. The next day, he went to his friend's widow to ask if he could look something up in his library. Though Jung was not acquainted with the library, everything was in place as it had been in his vision—the stool under the bookcase and the five books with red bindings. The title of the second book was *The Legacy of the Dead* by Emile Zola. The contents had no meaning or interest for Jung but in recalling the experience he said that, "Only the title was extremely significant in connection with this experience."

We can only speculate what Jung believed was so significant about the title. Perhaps one legacy of the dead is their ability (the source of which is unknown) to communicate with the living. Perhaps the message his friend wanted to get across was that his appearance, vision, or apparition—whatever we might call it—was real; that the dead live on. There was personal meaning for the living in Jung's vision of his friend.

Some critics challenge the idea that visionary messages of any type could be considered valid. They insist that the power of suggestion and expectancy on the part of the mourner is the catalyst behind why one sees the deceased. Although a host of visual experiences occur when the mourner is not thinking of the return of the loved one, it is difficult to explain away experiences in which the deceased speaks and gives advice.

Judy Tatelbaum, in *The Courage to Grieve*, provides an excellent illustration of a woman whose deceased father appeared at the foot of her bed on several occasions, and each time was laughing. This was disturbing to her, and when trying to figure out why he was laughing ". . . she suddenly 'heard' him say as he might have when alive, 'Laugh a little. Don't take this grief so seriously.'" Thereafter her father's visitations ended.

What Is the Meaning of the Visual Experience?

For an outsider looking in, perhaps the most intriguing question to be asked is "What is the meaning of these unbidden appearances of the deceased to the living?" Certainly, the question has been asked many times. . . . Most survivors who experience the deceased loved one believe the answer is quite obvious: their loved ones are very concerned about how they are adjusting to their deaths. They want their survivors to realize they are all right and to accept their deaths. Certainly, this is not unreasonable. It could very well be their task to draw the living into greater love for each other as well as to say "our love is eternal even though we are separated." In this realm, the deceased are very much concerned about the living and their relationships. Perhaps the deceased, by their appearances, are attempting to alert their loved ones not to be discouraged, that there is a much broader meaning to existence, and that "we will meet again." For many survivors, the thought that they will someday be with their loved ones—based on the interpretation of their visual experiences—is a powerful ally in the management of grief. They receive a feeling of empowerment which transcends any sense of isolation or abandonment.

A Ghost Investigation

Joshua P. Warren

In their efforts to prove conclusively that ghosts exist, some ghost hunters have turned to technology. They use normal and infrared photography, tape recorders, electromagnetic detectors, thermal imaging, and other simple and sophisticated tools to measure atmospheric conditions and various kinds of energy. They hope these tools will enable them to catch and analyze anomalies. Ghost hunters also study weather conditions, water tables, and how a building settles to try to eliminate every possible normal physical cause of ghostly effects. If some effects cannot be explained, there may be proof of a ghost.

Ghost hunter Joshua P. Warren, along with three friends, visited a hotel in Asheville, North Carolina, that is famous for its ghost, the Pink Lady. In the following selection, Warren gives his account of their investigation.

From "In Search of the Pink Lady," by Joshua P. Warren, *FATE*, June 1997. Copyright © 1997 by *FATE*. Reprinted with permission.

"Excuse me."

I snapped out of my little world of scientific readings and raised my gaze to the puzzled woman before me. She stared down with a wrinkled brow as I stooped beside an antique chair. "Yes?" I said.

"I don't mean to be nosy," she said, her head cocked to the side, "but I was wondering what sort of gadget that is."

I looked down at the electromagnetic field meter in my hand. To end her questions, I gave her the first conventional answer that came to mind. "It's a light meter," I said. I continued to take readings from the chair.

She was quiet for a few moments more before saying, "It doesn't look like a light meter to me."

I realized this woman wouldn't just go away. She was curious. There she was in the Grove Park Inn, the finest resort hotel in the Blue Ridge Mountains of North Carolina, and she had found a guy taking readings from a chair. You don't run across that sort of thing every day.

Remembering that the hotel wanted my work done as confidentially as possible, I was slow to tell her the truth. "Well, there have been some—how should I put it—strange goings-on in the Grove Park Inn."

Her eyes brightened and her smile beamed. "You're looking for ghosts, aren't you?" she asked.

"You might say that."

She grew even more excited. "Tell me all about it!" she exclaimed.

I sat down beside her, and, after making it very clear that there was much I could not discuss, I told the story of the Pink Lady. It is, without a doubt, the most famous legend concerning the classic hotel. Built in Asheville by E.W. Grove in 1913, the Grove Park Inn has seen more famous faces than one can easily list by memory. From Thomas Edison, Henry Ford, and Franklin D. Roosevelt, to Richard Nixon, Dan Aykroyd, and a host of other celebrities, scholars, and politicians, the Grove Park Inn is not impressed by big names. There are lots of stories of guests here, but none of them are as popular as the one about the lady in pink.

The Pink Lady

On a chilly November night sometime in the late 1910s or early 1920s, a young woman wearing a long, pink gown was staying in the hotel. Her room was in the Palm Court, the core of the Main Inn, where six levels of rooms encircle a spacious drop to the lounge below. It is said that the young lady somehow fell to her death there. No one knows whether her fall was accident, murder, or suicide. Ever since the event supposedly occurred, however, employees and guests have been reporting unexplainable phenomena throughout the historic building.

Since the first documented occurrences around 1940, people have encountered everything from a pink phantom gliding through the hotel to a rash of mischievous and unexplainable events. Occurrences range from small events such as objects moving around, doors of vacant rooms being locked from the inside, elevators being buzzed to empty floors, and typewriters typing by themselves, to large events like bellmen being physically pushed by invisible forces and every guest room light in the empty hotel turning on at once.

The witness list includes people from all walks of life, from bellmen and maids, to doctors and chiefs of police. Although in the most extreme encounters, employees have quit their jobs and guests have been moved to different rooms, the occurrences are always benevolent. There has never been a malicious story attached to the elusive, and somewhat forlorn, phantom.

For years, hotel administration forbade its employees to

gossip about the ghostly encounters, unsure of how the public would react. In November 1995, however, the Grove Park Inn hired me to officially research the phenomena for the first time in history. My results were to appear in a media release about the Pink Lady. Rather than allowing the rumors to continue, the hotel decided to officially recognize the phenomena and make sure that they were accurately portrayed to the public.

This was as far as I got with the woman in the hotel lobby. The investigation was still pretty much under wraps at that point. She begged me for more details, as well as my results, but I held true to my pledge of secrecy. I was about to continue my work, when she said, "At least tell me this: Have you gotten any positive results yet?"

I looked back at her and replied, "Oh yes . . . ooooh yes." With that, I disappeared into a crowd moving toward a wing of the hotel. I didn't look back, but I knew that I had driven her crazy.

Tools

I had been studying that chair in the lobby for a reason. At approximately 5:30 A.M., on December 30, 1995, I had captured a strange image in a photograph of the chair. Using Kodak 1000 speed film and a 35mm camera, I had inadvertently snapped a photo of a gray mist hovering over the chair. At the time the photograph was taken, there was no visible indication of an apparition, and no instrumentation was in use. After the photo was developed, it was examined by four photographic experts. None of them could give me a conventional explanation for the image.

In addition to our 35mm cameras (some of them able to photograph in the infrared and ultraviolet range), I and my colleagues Mark-Ellis Bennett, Tim Vandenberghe, and Tim Pedersen used devices such as ultra- and subsonic audio recording equipment, a night-vision scope, electromagnetic field detectors, a video camera, a Wimshurst generator, a Van de Gram generator, and a Tesla coil. It is my belief that spectral materialization is achieved by a high concentration of electrical ions (accompanied by fluctuating electromagnetic fields). Devices such as the Wimshurst and Van de Graff generators produce a great number of ions and were sometimes employed with the hope of enhancing ghostly activity. Of course, the Tesla coil can be used to manipulate the electrical environment in a number of ways.

Though my colleagues worked with me at irregular intervals, I ultimately stayed in a total of 20 rooms at the Grove Park Inn over a period of ten nights between December 29, 1995, and May 27, 1996. During this time, we took five photographs (four with 35mm 1000 speed film and one ultraviolet photograph) that contained some sort of unexplainable image. When we took the photographs, we often detected a strong, fluctuating electromagnetic field.

From the start it was apparent that the Grove Park Inn was highly conducive to supernatural activity. Strong, fluctuating electromagnetic energy fields (sometimes up to 8 milligauss, the amount found one inch from a television screen) randomly passed through secluded areas of the massive granite structure and then mysteriously disappeared. Although we tried to find conventional sources for the energy, in most cases we were unsuccessful.

Strange Energies

Over the course of the investigation, two events significantly affected our research. The first one began on the afternoon of January 4, 1996. Mark-Ellis Bennett (a specialist in infrared and ultraviolet photography, as well as audio recording) noticed something odd about a photograph made the night of December 29, 1995. It was a photograph of Tim

Pedersen and me standing on the fifth floor of the Palm Court. We posed for the photo (taken by an elevator operator) simply to commemorate our first night of research. In the background of the photograph, however, an unusual orange glow appeared outside room 545. Bennett felt the room should be investigated, and I wholeheartedly agreed.

We tried to enter room 545 with the maid's key—a credit card type key passed through an electronic slot—but the door would not open. After several more tries, the door still would not unlock. Next, we obtained the guest key. Once again the door wouldn't open after several tries.

We eventually had to have security personnel open the door. Once inside, we detected massive fluctuating energy fields throughout the room. Bennett and I decided to come back that night with the equipment necessary to conduct formal research. However, upon our return, the activity had died down.

The next night, after midnight, I returned to room 545 with Mark-Ellis Bennett and Tim Vandenberghe. We set up the electromagnetic field meter on the arm of a chair and observed it from a distance. We patiently watched it for quite a while, but the meter read little or no energy. Suddenly, the meter detected a small energy gain, which grew and began to fluctuate. We fired away with our cameras and after a few moments, Bennett rushed to the site and held his hand over the meter. He exclaimed that he felt a strange sensation on the surface of his skin. Vandenberghe and I raced over and held out our hands as well. At first I felt nothing. Then I suddenly experienced one of the strangest sensations of my life.

An unexplainable feeling of weight pressed down on my hand and the hair on my knuckles stood up. The force felt full of static but neutral in temperature. After a few seconds it was gone, and Vandenberghe exclaimed, "I feel it!" Then it left his hand as well. We all described experiencing the same sensations. After that, the energy in the room seemed to die down.

By the end of our investigation, I concluded that room 545 was the most supernaturally active room in the hotel.

The night of January 20, 1996, marked another major event in the investigation. Tim Vandenberghe and I had set up a Van de Graff generator in Elaine's, the hotel's night-club. There had been countless sightings in the club, and we regularly picked up strong readings there. After the generator ran a few moments, it began dispersing electrical discharges of approximately four inches. Vandenberghe viewed the scene through an infrared night-vision scope.

After approximately thirty minutes, the electrical discharges from the generator began to grow in size. They reached a peak of a little over one foot long and then branched out in midair, as though they were drawn to some invisible conductor. I took many photographs, and Vandenberghe continued to use his scope while lying on his back and looking upward. This continued for a while, and then the activity seemed to lessen in intensity.

When I returned to the scene later, Vandenberghe, his face pale and his eyes large, said, "I saw something!" He claimed that while lying on his back, he had seen a white streak of illumination. Eager to rule out a conventional cause, we reproduced the circumstances, watching for reflections and light sources. After two attempts, we could not recreate the effect. We found no natural explanation for what he claimed to see.

I was amazed when I later developed the photographs from that night. A photo of the generator, made only ten minutes before the sighting, showed a white streak of illumination in the upper right-hand corner. Vandenberghe claims to have seen something very similar.

Although paranormal activities can and do take place all over the hotel, by the end of the field research, I had pinpointed the two most active sites in the hotel. By *active* I mean sites having the highest potential to host a paranormal experience. These two sites are the fifth floor of the hotel (particularly room 545) and Elaine's nightclub. If the legendary Pink Lady died from a fall, it's likely she stayed in room 545 and fell from the fifth floor balcony outside her room.

Mystery Unsolved

Though I interviewed a number of people and searched through many records, I was not able to uncover the identity of the Pink Lady. The Grove Park has virtually no guest records until recent times.

If the Pink Lady died in a fall, the tragedy may have been kept secret. When asked a previous hotel employee if anyone had died in the hotel, she replied, "I imagine if anyone did die, they slipped them outta there without letting the employees know. It's not one of those things that they would advertise."

During our investigation, we did confirm that strange things are happening at the Grove Park Inn. The identity of the Pink Lady, however, remains an enigma.

Why Ghosts Look the Way They Do

Hilary Evans

Ghosts have two common types of appearance, says Hilary Evans, the author of the following selection. They either wear long robes (the Halloween ghost-in-a-sheet type), or they look like normal human beings wearing the clothing they wore in their lifetime. Evans suggests that ghosts choose these appearances because they want to be recognized. Evans is a longtime researcher of paranormal topics and the author of several books.

The year is 1940. Mr. Frank Clifton, a citizen of Brownsville, Texas, is honeymooning with his bride in a hotel in Mexico. In the middle of the night he wakes, and is astonished to see a nude lady with long hair kneeling beside the bed. His first thought is that his newly acquired wife—who herself has long hair—has got out of bed in the middle of

Excerpted from "The Naked Ghost," by Hilary Evans, *The Anomalist*, Winter 1995. Copyright © 1995 by *The Anomalist*. Reprinted with permission.

the night to pray, though why she should wish to do so he cannot imagine. He promptly suggests that she should come back to bed—whereupon the figure vanishes, and he realizes that his wife has been sleeping soundly beside him throughout the incident. The following day, talking with the hotel proprietor, Frank learns he is not the first guest to have been visited at night by the mysterious figure; others have reported a similar vision.

Ghost stories of this kind are commonplace—except for one feature: nude ghosts are surprisingly rare. Indeed, Frank Clifton's experience is so exceptional as to be almost unique. Most ghosts come wrapped.

Yet if ghosts are what they are generally supposed to be, visitors from another realm of being, this is rather strange. We might think that in the next world the spirits will have abandoned the use of clothes, with all their inconveniences. We mortals have hedged ourselves around with all kinds of taboos restricting the degree to which we reveal to others parts of our bodies which everyone knows we possess. But surely such ridiculous restrictions will not apply in the next world, which we have the right to expect will be culturally more advanced than ours?

One possible answer is that, yes indeed, those who have passed on to another world have shed their inhibitions—and their clothing along with them. But when occasions require them to undertake a return visit to earth, they remember how shocked we humans are at the sight of naked bodies, so they put their clothes on again (fortunately not having destroyed them, but having kept them stored safely in the attic on the principle of you never know when they may come in handy) so as not to offend our earthly sensibilities.

Be that as it may, it is a fact that ghosts are usually clothed. However, this seemingly trivial observation leads to some more profound speculations which carry us to the heart of the question which mankind has been asking itself for a couple of millennia and more: what are ghosts, and why do they manifest as they do? . . .

The History of a Stereotype

How did the popular image of the ghost come into being? That isn't a difficult question to answer, as soon as we remind ourselves what ghosts are popularly supposed to be: that is, persons who were once living on earth like ourselves, but who have now passed on to some other plane of existence, from which they can—if the conditions are right—return to revisit the land of the living.

That being the case, a childlike logic suggests that naturally they will wear the clothes they were buried in, for all their other clothes were left behind on earth (thus putting paid to our hypothesis about spirits in the next world keeping their terrestrial clothing in the attic; but don't worry, we can easily figure a way round that one, like for instance how about the clothes aren't real clothes but imaginary ones reconstructed out of ectoplasm or something?).

In ancient times folks were generally put in their graves wearing a shroud or winding-sheet, consequently this is what the earliest ghosts habitually wore. So when we see depictions of the souls of Breton dead being ferried to their final resting-place in the Fortunate Isles, or of the Roman dead brought from their graves by the power of the full moon, we see them dressed in their burial shrouds.

And this is true, not only of general folk-belief, but in specific cases. One of the oldest ghost stories took place in October, 42 BC, on the eve of the battle of Philippi. Brutus, one of those responsible for assassinating Julius Caesar, is meditating in his tent when the ghost of his victim appears and predicts his death the following day. What is Caesar wearing? Naturally, the winding-sheet he was buried in.

In the following century another ghost appearance led to the first recorded instance of psychical investigation. Plinius the Younger tells us how the philosopher Athenodorus purchased a house which was being sold cheap because it was said to be haunted. One night he was visited by the resident ghost who led him to a specific spot in the garden, where buried bones were discovered, presumably those of the victim. Once again, Athenodorus' ghost is wearing the clothes he was buried in.

Many centuries later, in 1779, the wicked English nobleman, Lord Lyttleton, is in bed at night when there appears in his bedroom the ghost of the dead mother of two sisters, both of whom he has seduced. She has come to warn him that by the time the clock strikes midnight, he will join her in the grave; and it is the clothes of the grave that she is wearing. (Of course it goes without saying that he did indeed drop dead at the predicted hour . . .)

The tradition continues to more recent times. At Buntingford, England, in 1931, some country lads take to their heels when they see a ghost drifting mysteriously across some marshes. Telling their story, they report that the figure was dressed in long, trailing garments . . .

Indeed, we may wonder if any of these witnesses would have been believed, if they had described their ghost in any other way? For the consensus image of ghosts serves a useful social function: it means that when anyone uses the word "ghost," all his hearers will instantly conjure up a mental picture of what he is talking about. And if the image is also a logical one—what else would ghosts returning from the tomb be expected to wear?—that surely explains why ghosts appear as they do.

Or so it would, except that we must now confront a very disconcerting paradox which seems to make nonsense of the popular stereotype.

A Paradox

The fact is that real-life ghosts, as opposed to those of legend and folklore, do not as a rule conform to the stereotype. Instead, "true" ghosts prefer to appear dressed in the clothes they wore during their lifetime, rather than the ones they were buried in. In fact, such ghosts are often impossible to distinguish from living people, so that in many cases the witness is under the illusion that he is seeing the actual individual, not his ghostly spirit.

Probably the famous collection of true-life ghost stories is the collection *Phantasms of the Living*, gathered towards the end of the 19th century by the London Society for Psychical Research (SPR). It contains many hundreds of stories, honestly reported and, wherever possible, independently confirmed. Yet virtually every one of them describes a phantasm of normal appearance and dressed in everyday clothing: you will search the pages in vain for the traditional shrouded figure with outstretched arms, the clanking chains and the wailing cries.

Typical of the cases reported to the SPR is that of Kathleen Leigh-Hunt. In 1884 she was staying in a house in Hyde Park Place, London. One day she was walking up the stairs when, to her surprise, she became aware that one of the housemaids was walking before her. Just as they reached the top of the stairs, the maid vanished; yet until that point the figure had seemed so lifelike that Kathleen had supposed it to be a real servant. No explanation was ever forthcoming as to who the phantom maid had been and why she manifested in this way.

It would, however, be a mistake to think that the change from traditional "ghost-like" ghosts to "real-life" ghosts is a simple consequence of our increasingly rational way of looking at things. A century or more before Kathleen's experience with the housemaid, at about the same time that Lord Lyttleton was receiving his fatal warning, an English household were discussing the future of the family estate. Alexander, the eldest son, had gone to India, and nothing had been heard from him for five years; his stepmother, who wished to pass the family estates to her own children, insisted he must be dead. But then, in the middle of the discussion, his face was seen at the window: "Here," said the spectre of Alexander. Five months later, the son returned to England in person: he was astonished to learn that he had been preceded by his own ghost. But what his family saw was not a ghostbuster-type wraith, but Alexander's true likeness.

It might be argued that one reason why ghosts are more often seen in real-life clothes is simply that today people are not often buried in winding sheets; more likely it will be in their own clothes. Even so, it will be special clothes—a fine dress, a smart suit, whereas ghosts are generally reported as being in typical everyday clothing.

In one of the most striking cases investigated by the Society for Psychical Research, an English priest, Canon Phillips, was sitting at home watching television one evening in 1964: he was undergoing some mental stress at the time, and this crisis in his affairs was surely the reason for his experience. Suddenly he became aware that a well-known writer, C.S. Lewis, who had recently died, was sitting in another chair a meter or so away. Lewis gave him a reassuring message.

Phillips had not known Lewis well, but was able to describe him in detail—including his clothing: the ghost was wearing a thick suit which was characteristic of the living man. Yet on the only occasion Phillips and the living C.S. Lewis had actually met, Lewis had been wearing ecclesiastical clothing, so it could not have been a simple act of memory on Phillips part which caused the ghost to appear as it did.

Because of the circumstances, and being an intelligent man, Phillips realised immediately that his companion was a ghost and adjusted his mental set accordingly. But there are times when the fact is not so obvious. In Denver, Colorado, in the 1890s, a young office-worker named Stella Dean was asked by one of her work colleagues, Vera Cummings, "Who is that tall, good-looking girl, Stella, that I've seen following you into the building on several occasions?" Stella insisted she had always been alone: but Vera's description of the figure she had seen matched another colleague, Hester Holt, who had disappeared mysteriously a few weeks earlier and whom Vera had never met. Later it was established that Stella had in fact killed Hester out of jealousy.

Two Types of Ghost?

When we consider this selection of cases, it seems as though there must be two separate and distinct types of ghost. On the one hand, there are what we may call the Folklore Society's ghosts: this is the kind which appears in one of the traditional forms—the shadowy figure in the long trailing garment, phantom monks and nuns, and so on. On the other hand, by contrast, there are what we may call the Psychical Research Society's ghosts, which appear in a form so lifelike that often they are mistaken for living persons. . . .

Do ghosts exist when nobody is looking at them? That is a philosophical question which we have no means of answering: but even if we do not know why ghosts exist, we can adopt as a reasonable working hypothesis that their purpose is to be seen.

In which case, it is essential that they should be not only seen, but also recognized. This is well shown by another classic case, the Cheltenham hauntings.

The main occurrences took place between 1882–1889, in a large private residential house owned by the Despard family. A tall woman in black, often holding a handkerchief to her face, was seen by at least seventeen people. Her footsteps were heard by twenty witnesses, and twice she was sensed by animals—the family dog ran to the foot of the stairs, wagging its tail and jumping up as if greeting someone: then slunk away with its tail between its legs to hide under a sofa, trembling.

The primary witness was 19-year-old medical student Rosina Despard. She tried on several occasions to catch the ghost, but was never successful: she placed fine threads across the staircase, but twice she saw the figure pass through her threads without moving or breaking them. Once Rosina spoke to the figure, but it gave only a slight gasp, moved away and vanished.

Most ghosts manifest only at night: the Cheltenham ghost was seen both by night and in bright sunlight. Most are seen only for a moment: this one would stand in full view for up to half an hour. Most manifest only indoors: this was seen in the garden and the orchard also. Most are seen only by members of the family or by close friends: this was seen also by servants, visitors and strangers.

Because it was seen so often and so clearly, it was possible to make a fairly confident identification. Rosina's inquiries led to a tentative conclusion that their household ghost was an earlier resident, Imogen Swinhoe, the unhappily married second wife of the house's first owner.

We can only speculate why the ghost should have manifested almost wholly during the occupancy of the Despard family. Because Rosina was the one who saw it most frequently, there is a possibility that some kind of rapport was generated between her and the ghost, giving it the power to appear. However, there have been subsequent sightings, some as recently as 1985. One of the most striking took place in 1970, when a Mrs. Jackson, taking a driving lesson, was just passing the house when a tall woman in black, holding her hand to her face, stepped out into the path of the car. Mrs. Jackson was forced to brake sharply, yet her driving instructor had seen nothing.

The mechanism of ghost-seeing is still a matter for conjecture. However, many believe that the experience of seeing a ghost involves not one but two active participants, the percipient and the apparent. A favored view is that ghosts are not wholly autonomous, but in part (at least) contingent upon a contribution made by the percipient's subconscious mind. That is why we are not all of us seeing ghosts all of the time: we have to be the right kind of person, or in the right physical circumstances, or in the right state of mind.

As to why ghosts manifest, there may be many reasons. But in some cases, if not all, they seem to have a definite purpose—to convey information, or a warning, or somehow make up for something done or not done during their lifetime. If so, identification of the ghost is all-important. In the case of Stella Dean of Denver, it was crucial that the ghost of Hester should be recognised—she had to appear in her own clothes, and looking like her living self, otherwise her identity would never have been revealed and her murderer would have gone unpunished. Clearly, recognition is obviously a key factor in many ghost visitations. It is safe to conclude that the need to be identified provides the clue to many puzzling aspects of ghosts, spirits and other entities.

Somehow, those responsible for creating the ghost—and if we are correct in saying that it takes two to make a ghost, this means the percipient as well as the apparent—must effect a balance between establishing the nature of the ghost—that is, making it obvious to the percipient that what s/he is seeing is a ghost—and establishing the identity of the ghost as an individual.

Recognizing this dual necessity helps us to understand why some ghosts take the form of "Folklore Society" ghosts and others of "Psychical Research Society" ghosts.

It also explains why we do not see many naked ghosts.

Chapter 2

Ghosts Are
Not Real

Belief in Ghosts Is Merely Self-Deception

Bertram Rothschild

There are times when even those who do not believe in ghosts are alarmed by seemingly mysterious ghostly activity. This happened to the author of the following selection. Confirmed skeptic and clinical psychologist Bertram Rothschild tells how one mysterious little incident almost made him reconsider his disbelief in ghosts. But when he forced himself to think about the situation rationally, he realized that he was allowing his imagination to rule his thoughts. Rothschild believes many people deceive themselves this way.

For a while, I (almost) believed a ghost occupied my house. Before I confess all, however, you need to know something about me. First, I'm approaching (not there yet) my dotage;

From "The Ghost in My House: An Exercise in Self-Deception," by Bertram Rothschild, *The Skeptical Inquirer*, January 2001. Copyright © 2001 by The Committee for the Scientific Investigation of Claims of the Paranormal. Reprinted with permission.

second, I'm a clinical psychologist; and third, I was a skeptic well before I knew the word, much less its meaning. If asked about ESP and the spirit world, I would laugh and wonder about what kind of idiot could believe such things. The arguments I've had with believers sometimes almost led to blows, though in my later decades I decided that keeping my mouth shut was wise. But, with further maturity, I concluded that the wisest course of action would be to focus my skepticism on issues of public concern.

Here's the story: I lay in bed one evening, half dozing, with the bedroom door shut. My wife gets to bed later than I do, but sometimes she'll come in to find something and then leave, again shutting the door. You must understand: this is a decades-old pattern, one with which I am quite familiar. Well, as I lay there, I heard her footsteps approaching the door. I saw the door open with exactly the same speed as always, and it opened to the same distance as usual. I expected to hear her footsteps coming into the room, but there was no such sound. (As I write this, I realize that I did not hear her footsteps. It was an after-the-fact embellishment obviously supportive of the ghost theory.)

My first assumption was that she had changed her mind, but two considerations suggest otherwise. First, she would have closed the door, and second, there were no footsteps leading away. Okay, it wasn't her so it must have been a puff of wind. But the night was calm and no window was open. The puff of wind hypothesis dissolved.

A Ghost?

Now in some consternation, I arose and looked for her. She was not in a nearby room, not anywhere on the bedroom level. I walked further to the little balcony that overlooks the downstairs area and there I saw her, with a bowl of cereal and thoroughly ensconced in a crossword puzzle. Although the circumstances convinced me it could not have been her, I asked. She denied having anything to do with the door that had mysteriously opened and went back to the puzzle. Although she has at times been a trickster, she would always give me a clue about her intent to tease me. Without a triumphant grin on her face, she clearly had not tried to disconcert me.

When I described the door's peculiar behavior she jokingly asked if I thought it were a ghost. I snickered at her and returned to bed. A ghost? Ridiculous. I soon fell asleep. The next morning, dozing in bed, I became aware of the noises—and she did too. One of us said: "Perhaps it was the ghost." We both laughed, but we both listened for more strange sounds. And, of course, they were there.

That evening, in the den watching television, we both heard sort of a combined clink and thud clearly indicating that some hard object had fallen to the floor. I examined the area and could find nothing to account for the sound. Were we disquieted? You bet. The noises continued over several days, and we jokingly got into the habit of evoking the ghost as explanation . . . and I started to take that explanation seriously. As a consequence, the hairs on my arms would stand up when I could not find an explanation for some sound or event.

At the same time, I resisted the "ghost" explanation and wondered about my willingness to accept the possibility. The noises, after all, were really nothing new, just the creaks and groans of the house. They had always been there, but rarely the focus of my attention. Either every house I'd ever visited had a resident ghost (possible, but surely unlikely), or house noises were commonplace, not the production of invisible spirits. But the door incident remained on my mind. I realized, finally, that my mind, operating out of awareness, demanded an explanation of the door's behavior. It wasn't the wind; it wasn't my wife. What the hell was it? I had to know; but only the ghost hypothesis remained.

Let Go of the Need for an Explanation

Because of my training as a Rational-Emotive Behavior Therapist (REBT) I had learned to challenge the notion of demandingness. After some mental work on that I finally realized that I didn't have to know what prompted the door to open; once I achieved that, I stopped fixating on the damned (no irony intended) event. I had made the same error that humans have made since our cave-dwelling ancestors roamed the earth. When rational explanation failed to settle the matter, they invoked spirits and magical events. Any explanation would be better than chaos and, if one could invoke the spirits, it implied power over ugly reality. And we are the genetic inheritors of what worked for survival.

Albert Ellis (the creator of REBT), a highly esteemed psychologist, has suggested that human beings 1) have a strong tendency to be irrational, and 2) have a strong tendency to ignore data contrary to their beliefs. However, this can be overcome by training in critical thinking. That is the essence of his psychotherapy, teaching people how to think about their beliefs regarding reality. We need to teach our children how to think and reason at the earliest age possible, a process that should be ongoing.

No, I don't believe that a ghost opened the door, but that I had entertained the possibility continues to astonish me. Without an understanding of the event, my brain simply created a magical explanation despite my years of looking at the universe in a rational way. We all do that. Our brains fill in the blanks, and without considerable debunking effort we fall prey to such "explanations." Children do this all the time; and for many people nothing changes with age—they continue to explain events with their idiosyncratic construction of explanations that have nothing to do with reality.

When I was a child, I asked my mother to tell me how lightning and thunder are produced. She explained that clouds bumped into each other, producing a spark and noise. I won't tell you how old I was before I figured it out. But, how many more subtle explanations have I (or you) lived by, never noticing their absurdity?

If we embark on such an enterprise, educators had better anticipate a negative reaction from parents. Many parents would become enraged with children who come home and puncture their beliefs. Enraged parents become profoundly interested in their school boards, and school boards often cave in to placate them. An example occurred not so long ago in Colorado. A town put up a library with gargoyles on it as ornaments. Upset parents demanded that they be removed because gargoyles "represent the devil." Explanations of the churchly history of gargoyles did not change their minds and the gargoyles came down.

So, yes, let's see if we can't get the schools to provide some training in how to think and reason. That it will be a difficult battle is of no consequence.

(Shh! I'm trying to figure out what happens to socks that disappear in the dryer. Can it be . . . ?)

The Columbus Poltergeist Was a Fake

James Randi

Poltergeists are usually associated with a "focus person"; that is, the events happen in a particular person's presence or seem to be directed at a particular person. Often, the focus person is a teenager. In Columbus, Ohio, in 1984, a classic poltergeist case occurred. The focus person, Tina Resch, was fourteen and had emotional problems beyond those of the typical teen: She was struggling with her identity as an adopted child, she was hyperactive, and she had been removed from her regular school because of problems there.

Over a period of several months, many strange and apparently unexplainable events occurred around Tina. Many of these incidents involved flying objects, including telephones, lamps, books, and other items. Tina's family and

Excerpted from "The Columbus Poltergeist Case: Flying Phones, Photos, and Fakery," by James Randi, *The Outer Edge: Classic Investigations of the Paranormal*, edited by Joe Nickell, Barry Karr, and Tom Genoni (Amherst, NY: The Committee for the Scientific Investigation of Claims of the Paranormal, 1996). Copyright © 1996 by The Committee for the Scientific Investigation of Claims of the Paranormal. Reprinted with permission.

others were convinced that a poltergeist had invaded the Resch home. The Columbus newspaper photographer managed to catch several flying objects on film. Soon, the story was known around the world, and it attracted a number of investigators, including James Randi.

Randi does not believe that poltergeists exist. He is a professional magician and a prominent member of the Committee for the Scientific Investigation of Claims of the Paranomal, an organization devoted to the scientific study of alleged paranormal events. Randi has spent the last several decades debunking paranormal claims. As he indicates in the following selection, he did not have the opportunity to investigate the Columbus poltergeist firsthand, but he did find sufficient evidence to convince him that Tina Resch's poltergeist was not real.

March 1984 came in like a lion at the home of John and Joan Resch in the North Side district of Columbus, Ohio. Reporters who were called in to witness the evidence found broken glass, dented and overturned furniture, smashed picture frames, and a household in general disarray. The focus of all this activity seemed to be 14-year-old Tina, an adopted child who had shared the Resch home with some 250 foster children who came and went over the years.

Tina, a hyperactive and emotionally disturbed girl who had been taken out of school and was being privately tutored through the Franklin County Children's Services (FCCS), was interviewed by every media outlet who could get near the two-story frame house where these poltergeist activities were claimed to be taking place. Every day the street outside was jammed with vans and cars stuffed with television crews, reporters, and photographers who joyously tumbled over one another in their enthusiasm for what had become a circus.

Mike Harden, a reporter for the *Columbus Dispatch*, was the first on the scene. He had written an article on the Resch family some five months before, praising their work with foster children. He was aware that Tina was trying to trace her true parents against the wishes of Mr. and Mrs. Resch, who felt it was not a good idea. One of their other adopted children had found his parents, and it did not turn out very well. In view of his previous encounter with the Resches, Harden considered himself a friend of the family.

During that first big press conference at the Resch home, more than forty persons were jammed into a 20' × 20' room. Participants described it to me as "rude" and "typically media." Comments from reporters we interviewed were:

"We didn't listen to what each of us was saying. We just jumped in." There was "no development of questions."

"We tried to find the truth. We're obviously not equipped to do it."

"It would have been much more comfortable with two teams—or three."

"It was a complete free-for-all."

"We were on her like flies on flypaper."

"Our attention was constantly diverted. When a reporter knocked something over by accident and took the blame for it, there was general disappointment."

A Poltergeist?

Although the older Resches denied any prior belief in supernatural matters, they soon agreed that such goings-on probably resulted from a "poltergeist." This translates as, "noisy spirit" though some of the slightly less naive parapsychologists tend to ascribe these events to psychokinesis (PK) rather than ghosts. Since the record of past cases indicates that when these destructive phenomena take place very frequently an unhappy adolescent is in the vicinity and they cease when the youngster is recognized and satisfied, explanations other than supernatural ones immediately suggest themselves.

On March 5, photographer Fred Shannon, a 30-year veteran on the *Dispatch* staff, accompanied reporter Mike Harden to the Resch house to try to catch the elusive poltergeist events on film. By his own admission, Shannon was "afraid" of what might happen and was fully primed by Harden to witness miracles. During the first three hours of his visit, he took a remarkable series of photographs, but the actual story of how he and the public were apparently bamboozled by an adolescent girl is far more remarkable.

I have long believed that the major difference between the skeptic and the parapsychologist is one of expectation. The former does not believe that validation of paranormal claims is imminent; the latter depends upon that event for justification. Also, the skeptic will invoke parsimony—the simplest explanation consistent with the facts—where the parapsychologist eschews it. Personally, I find it much more reasonable, when objects fly about the room in the vicinity of an unhappy 14-year-old, to suspect poor reporting and observation rather than a repeal of the basic laws of physics.

It is true that the Committee for the Scientific Investigation of Claims of the Paranormal (CSICOP) was not invited to Columbus by the young lady at the center of these pranks, nor by her adoptive parents. But a call went out through the *Dispatch* for anyone who could help explain the phenomena. At that point CSICOP chairman Paul Kurtz contacted me and asked if I would join Case Western Reserve astronomers Steve Shore and Nick Sanduleak in Columbus to look into the case. I arrived on March 13 and was met by a mob of generally hostile reporters at the airport. The official CSICOP statement released to them at the interview expressed the hope that we would be admitted to the Resch home to look into the events first-hand.

Skeptical Randi Arrives but Is Kept Out

When I arrived in Columbus via Chattanooga, Tennessee, where I had been lecturing, and was joined there by the other two CSICOP investigators, I had no guarantee from the Resch family that we would be allowed to actually investigate anything. Upon reaching the house, Steve Shore asked Tina's parents whether we would be welcome. Mrs. Resch—as was her right, of course—said that the two astronomers could enter but not the "magician." She said it would be "sensationalizing" the matter to allow me access to the site. I did not see how she could honestly say that in view of the commotion brought about by the great number of press conferences and interviews that had taken place in the house. On one of those occasions there were, by actual count, more than 40 reporters, cameramen, and others rampaging about. The Resch case had become a major—though transitory—media event, featured all over the world.

But when we arrived the Resch home was already occupied by two investigators from the Psychical Research Foundation of Chapel Hill, North Carolina. William Roll and Kelly Powers had been enthusiastically welcomed to the house, and they had been living with the family for several days. Roll is the author of *The Poltergeist*, which [researcher] J.B. Rhine referred to as "a book on . . . what to do with a poltergeist until the parapsychologist comes."

When asked why I had been refused admittance to witness the events—and we specified that we wanted to go in *after* Roll and Powers, so as not to interfere with them—Mrs. Resch told reporters that Roll had insisted that I not be admitted. Roll denied this, saying that it was her ruling, not his. Later Mrs. Resch said, "We have a circus going already, and I don't need a magic show as well."

Roll said he would have let me in "if the conditions had been completely up to me, and if there had been no problem about the health situation." He was referring to Mr. Resch's recently elevated blood pressure. But reporter Dave Yost of the *Columbus Citizen Journal* told us that Roll had told him that he simply "didn't want Randi in there."

Following the departure of Roll and Powers, the Resch family told us they were leaving on a long vacation and would not be available for an interview with us. However, we discovered that they were still in their house two weeks after that announcement.

Amazing Photos

Because of the inaccessibility of the Resch home, the evidence we gathered centered around the film that was shot by photographer Shannon. One photo printed from the roll of 36 negatives (frame number 25) was published around the world as part of an Associated Press release. I had first become aware of the case from seeing the AP story in a Chattanooga newspaper. As a result of that one photo and its caption, much of the reading public now apparently believes that it represents a genuine example of either psychokinesis or spirit possession. This photo shows a telephone suspended in mid-air in front of Tina Resch while she cowers in fright. We called it "Attack of the Flying Killer Telephones" since the accompanying text said that the child was being assaulted regularly by these objects. The photo clearly shows that two telephones had been placed on the table at Tina's left side and that the handset of one of them is in motion in front of her. The cord is stretched out horizontally and shows transverse blurring.

Although it apparently had not occurred to any other investigators—including the parapsychologists—we asked to see the other 35 photos on that roll of film. We discovered seven flying telephones in all, and when the photographer admitted he had not been looking at the subject when taking the photographs, there was little mystery left.

Shannon had found that holding the camera to his eye and waiting for an event to occur was useless. It always seemed to happen just after he had relaxed and looked away. He referred to "The Force" when he spoke of the phenomenon. "It was tricky, and I would have to be tricky if I were to capture it on film. I decided I would outfox the force," he said. While Tina sat in a soft chair with two telephones within easy reach, Shannon looked away. When he saw a movement from the corner of his eye, he pressed the shutter. One result was the photo of Tina used by AP.

Now these photos were taken at $\frac{1}{125}$ of a second, using a strobe flash. Shannon used a wide-angle lens, of 24 mm focal length, which subtends an angle of 84 degrees. Further evidence of the wide-angle lens is seen in the distortion of objects and persons at the margins of each frame. (For comparison, a "normal" lens of 50 mm focal length covers only 45 degrees.) Thus the cameraman would have to be much closer to the subject than might be supposed from the wide area shown by each photograph. If Shannon was, as he has said, "turned away" from the subject, and yet seated as close as he apparently was, he could have had no appreciable perception of whatever action really took place. None of Shannon's photos was taken in rapid succession, since the strobe flash (a Vivitar) would not have recycled in time. Only one of them, number 25, was published worldwide. Recall that this classic photograph shows transverse movement of the telephone cord. The others do not. In one of the other flying-phone photos, frame number 30, it can be seen that this blurring took place along the length of the cord. Any blurring shown in the photos was a result of the film registering ambient room light (from the nearby window) since the strobe flash lasts about one-thousandth of a second, freezing almost any rapid action. The conclusion is obvious: Frame 25 shows that movement of the telephone was caused in a different fashion than was the movement in frames 24, 30, 31 and 32—those in which the telephones are actually frozen in flight. (Two others record the scene after the phone had fallen to the floor.)

Comparing Photos

What is different about the flying telephone in frame 25? Well, examination of frame 24, immediately preceding the photo published by the *Dispatch* and the AP, shows a strange situation. The phone cord is seen here already stretched out in front of Tina Resch, spanning the arms of the chair in which she is sitting, stationary, with the attached handset out of sight at her right, hanging down behind the side of the chair. Tina, typically, has her mouth open in a scream. (And there is a little girl—Miss "X"—standing and watching on the right. She was an eyewitness to this event and shows up in five other frames as well. We'll refer to her later.)

Simply by grabbing the phone cord at a spot near her right hand and yanking it hard, Tina could have caused the phone to fly up into exactly the position shown in the published photo, number 25. (We were able, at NBC-TV, to replicate this effect easily.) But looking at the other flying telephones that are revealed on the roll of film, we see longitudinal blurring, which indicates that Tina probably simply threw the telephone from camera right to camera left. In photo 12, Miss "X" is looking at the camera as if wondering whether that throw was convincing.

In photo 29, both telephones appear to have been in motion. Surely, it could be objected, if Tina simply tossed these phones around, she could not have tossed both of them without being caught at it! She surely would have been seen holding the phones, preparatory to throwing them when the "witnesses" were relaxed and looking away. A possible answer to this objection can be found when we examine frame 28, which shows Tina had a great deal of latitude in handling the equipment. She is freely holding the telephone apparatus in her hand while in animated conversation. It is evident that she, like other "psychics," is running the show her way, regardless of any requirements of security or control.

Frames 13, 22, and 28 show Tina similarly occupied, with the ubiquitous and mysterious Miss "X" once more present. During this entire photo session, it seems that an atmosphere of rather loose gaiety prevailed, but we are told that that's the only way these things are expected to take place. Reporter Harden shows up in four frames, numbers 14, 21, 22, and 23. He is, in every case, either obediently not watching Tina, so as not to inhibit her performance, or paging through a phone book.

But there is another frame, number 32, in which a new witness appears at the left edge of the photo during a flying-phone event. We asked the *Dispatch* to identify this woman, but got no help at all. Finally, through a reporter in Cincinnati, we learned that she was Lee Arnold, Tina's caseworker. We contacted Ms. Arnold by phone, and she told us that she had been instructed by her employers, Franklin County Children's Services, that if she gave any information about her witnessing the events she would be in danger of losing her job. She told us nothing.

And what of that other frequent witness, little Miss "X"? She remains a mystery. Obviously, she could reveal a great deal about Tina's actions during the time those photographs were being taken. But try as we may, no one will inform us how we may contact her. That is most unfortunate, since her testimony might reveal very interesting data.

It is the last of the flying telephones on Fred Shannon's film that really asks a great deal of our patience. It shows Tina Resch seated in the chair, her pointing left hand extended to her right across her body. The telephone cord is horizontally stretched out and the telephone handset is so far away as to be out of the frame altogether. Tina is in a stance suggestive of a major-league baseball player completing a throw to first base! Now, with the simple principle of parsimony in mind, we must ask ourselves if we will choose to believe that this is a photograph of a girl being affected by poltergeist activities or a photograph of a girl simply pitching a telephone across the room.

As I have said, the Resch household was inundated by the media. And, as luck would have it, Tina was caught cheating by them—though not by the parapsychologists who were the officially sanctioned investigators. On the only occasion that she believed she was not being observed electronically while television equipment was present, she was caught red-handed—twice—as can be seen in a news tape obtained accidentally by WTVN-TV, Channel 6 (ABC), Cincinnati. It happened at the end of a long press visit on March 8. The TV crew was packing up their equipment, but had left a camera aimed at Tina. Seated at one end of the sofa, near an end-table, and believing the camera was no longer active, she watched carefully until she was unobserved, then reached up and pulled a table-lamp toward herself, simultaneously jumping away, letting out a series of bleating noises, and feigning, quite effectively a reaction of stark terror. It matched other performances quite well. The lamp, on the first try, did not fall. Encouraged by the reaction, the girl then repeated the performance. This time, the lamp toppled to the floor. The TV crew hurried away to process their videotape for the next news broadcast, unaware that Tina's cheating had been recorded.

Discovering the imposture, WTVN-TV broadcast the tape, asking their viewers to make up their own minds about the event. Tina, confronted with the evidence after the broadcast, said coyly, and with much squirming about, that she was "only fooling" and did it because she wanted to get rid of the TV cameraman.

We may never see the rest of the TV tape as it was originally shown to the CSICOP team by WTVN-TV in their remote unit before it was edited. I pointed out to the TV crew at that time certain notable aspects of that tape and asked if I might have a complete copy of it. A copy was delivered to me, but I found that it consisted of only the portion that had been edited down for broadcast. When I asked about this I was told that I could not have the remainder, and when I reminded them of their promise to me they suddenly discovered that they had erased it—in error.

The missing portion of the videotape showed Tina Resch carefully and obviously setting up the trick. She edged around the sofa, glancing about her to be sure she was not being observed—not knowing the video camera on the floor was still connected, of course—and reaching up to test the height of the lamp shade. A moment later, thinking that she was safely unobserved, she is seen yanking at the shade and jumping away simultaneously, putting on her frightened act. Then she sets it up again and repeats the performance.

In frame number 20 of Fred Shannon's film, we see Tina doing the same trick. That same lamp falls in the same position, with her seated in the same place. Was this one, too, "only fooling"?

To take the edge off the cheating episode, after admitting that Tina had been caught, *Dispatch* reporter Mike Harden reassured his readers that WTVN-TV had witnessed a genuine miracle that same night: One of them had seen a table move mysteriously in the kitchen. But technician Robb Forest of WTVN told us that he'd caught Tina moving that table secretly with her foot, had accused her of it, and got only a horse-laugh from her for his trouble.

Irresponsible Media

Similarly, Mary Anne Sharkey (a good friend of Mike Harden) of the *Cleveland Plain-Dealer* reported to us—but not her readers—that Tina's obvious hanky-panky with a candlestick had disillusioned her on the story. She had been there with three other reporters, two photographers, and a TV crew when Tina pointed out to her a candlestick located in a plastic wreath under a table. Sharkey wondered why it had been pointed out. One hour later, after they had all moved about the house, Tina announced that the candlestick had vanished, and she began looking for it. With Sharkey following her around, Tina "found" it under a chair. Sharkey was unimpressed, but this did not become part of her story. Instead, she reported another episode that seemed more convincing.

NBC-TV news reporter Bill Wolfson, at first fascinated by Tina's performances, changed his mind after prolonged exposure to events, contradictory reports, and reconsideration of what he actually saw—or didn't see. As for the press conferences, he said, "I thought the tone and quality of questions were somewhat less than poor. They were provocative and leading. The media were going crazy. One reporter asked Tina, 'Don't you feel guilty?'" Wolfson finally summed it up for us as "bunk."

While he snapped frame number 26, photographer Shannon, as he looked elsewhere awaiting a miracle, must have believed that something "psychic" was happening. It shows the footrest at the base of a "recliner" chair in the extended position, and Tina looking startled—as if it had suddenly popped out. I have one of these chairs at home. To make the footrest protrude, one need only grasp the arms firmly and push back. This is the only photograph among the 36 in which Tina is holding the chair arms. Her startled expression would indicate to me only what she has proven in the past (as in the videotapes)—that she is an excellent actress.

The *Dispatch* naturally had a fine time with this story. One Sunday edition contained a huge spread on the subject. Two new photos were shown. One (frame 17) shows Tina holding an already-broken picture frame. One can clearly see that the glass is broken, and Tina is holding it like a tray, with the shards of glass retained on it. The following photo (18) shows her tilting it forward to dump the glass. But in that Sunday newspaper account, we see that the caption for the second photo says, "Below, the picture shatters in her hand and falls to the floor."

This is not a responsible representation at all. Reporter Dave Yost, who attended the Resch press conferences and followed Tina all the way to North Carolina when Bill Roll took her there for further observation, was frustrated by the attitude of the media. He said, "The real story here, I suspect, is the reaction of a duped media." Added Yost, "In spite of repeated efforts, I have never seen these reported events."

To return to the Shannon photos: In frame 21 (with reporter Harden studiously looking at the phone book at the right) we see a rollaway couch "jumping out" from the wall at Tina, who is again startled at another wonder of poltergeistry. But examination of a small lower section of a previous frame, this time taken from 90 degrees away with Tina standing in front of that couch holding an object for photographer Shannon, reveals an interesting fact: Tina clearly has her right foot hooked under the edge of the couch! A sudden pull backwards and the couch would "jump out" at her easily. We don't know if that is how it was done when she was later "attacked" by the couch. But there is ample evidence here to believe that it might have happened that way, and none to show that it did not.

Failed Investigation on All Sides

Admittedly, our team was not able to conduct a proper investigation of the Columbus poltergeist case. We were barred from the house and we never interviewed the girl involved. We could not trace one of two eyewitnesses to the photographed events, and the other witness was forbidden to tell us what she knew.

Witnesses we could identify were less than cooperative. Barbara Hughes, a neighbor and good friend of the Resch family and also a foster parent, spoke briefly with Steve Shore by phone, but refused to meet with us. She claimed to have seen one phenomenon while in the house. She said she addressed "The Force" out loud, demanding a demonstration. Something "fell," and she fled in terror. Drew Hadwal, working with WTVN-TV, "saw three chairs move apart" in the kitchen, we were told. I tried hard to reach him, but though the receptionist at Channel 6 said she knew he was in, when I gave my name over the telephone I was told that he was not going to be at work that day. Even electrician Bruce Claggett failed to return our calls and, although he was scheduled to be on the program with me at the annual meeting of the Parapsychological Association, he failed to appear.

Several reporters we did interview told us of damning details they had observed but never reported. One expressed his anger at the rewrite artists who had "fluffed up" his stories to the point where they were hyperbolic. The *Columbus*

Dispatch gave endless excuses why we could not meet Fred Shannon to discuss the evidence with him during our stay in Columbus, and reporter Harden eventually was "out" to us when we tried to call on him.

On the other hand Bill Roll actually stayed at the Resch house. He stated his professional conclusions twice during a press conference before taking Tina off to his lab in Chapel Hill. He said that, based upon stories told by witnesses, neurological and psychological tests of Tina, and his own experiences (during a half-hour period in the last hour of the last day of three he spent in residence) "when I felt I had Tina under close observation" he concluded that she had demonstrated "genuine recurrent spontaneous psychokinesis (RSPK)." Then he admitted that though he was "impressed . . . we are not dealing here with a controlled study, [but it was] sufficiently suggestive of RSPK." He added that his research was "in a very preliminary stage" and that he had come to "no definite conclusions."

Roll's evidence is based on a very short term of observation, with no other witnesses present and no direct experience of any event—only peripheral observations. His data consists of uncorroborated witnessing of a very few events, which he admits took place out of his direct line of sight at times when he was unable to anticipate them.

Questionable Witness Account

This is how he reported the events to the press conference: Immediately prior to the rush of phenomena, Tina had spent some 30 minutes upstairs, alone (only the two of them, so far as he knew, were in the house). Then she appeared at the top of the stairs screaming for him to rush up there and see miracles. A bar of soap, he reported, fell into the bathtub. Next, while they both were standing four feet from it, facing away, a picture fell from the wall. The nail had been pulled out of the wall. Roll and Tina rushed to it. Roll hammered the nail back with a pair of pliers. During this process, his small tape-recorder, which had been placed nearby on a dresser flew to a position seven feet away. Roll and Tina went to it, Roll leaving the pliers behind. The pliers "moved from the dresser" to hit the wall near him.

Roll described his own observing abilities in such a way that we must place his performance in the paranormal category. Or, at the very least, he had to have rather remarkable sensory powers. Consider (a) He was hammering a nail back into a wall using the edge of a pair of pliers (he called them "tongs")—an act that requires undivided attention, obviously; (b) he was "watching Tina carefully" (contrast this with his statement that he "felt he had Tina under close observation") and remember that the "possessed" girl was standing off to one side of him; and (c) he saw the tape machine fly away from a position directly behind him—a remarkable feat indeed, especially when the layout of the room is known.

Questioned, he admitted he had not once seen any object in place as it began to move. I postulate that, since he could not see the tape recorder, Tina had ample opportunity to throw it along the dresser, from which position it fell to the floor. Then she picked up the pliers as the two of them went to recover the tape recorder and threw them against the far wall as Roll examined the recorder. It was an assumption on his part that the pliers "moved from the dresser." He said, "She wasn't doing anything with her hands that I could see." (Roll is myopic and wears thick glasses; he is a poor observer.)

An examination of the videotape made in that room shows that the dresser on which the tape recorder sat was directly behind Roll as he faced the picture on the wall! He could not have seen it move. It is an impossible scenario.

Tina's Motives

But why would Tina Resch want to smash up her home and allow others to believe it was a paranormal event? Factors are found here that suggest strong motivation on her part to create a sensation. She was admittedly under stress and had good reason to want to attract media exposure: she wanted to trace her true parents, against the wishes of the Resches. And her "best friend," Missy Johnson, had a fight with her and broke off their friendship two days before the phenomena began. She was a girl looking for attention. And she got it.

The evidence for the validity of poltergeist claims in this case is anecdotal and thin, at best. The evidence against them is, in my estimation, strong and convincing.

Ed and Lorraine Warren Are Misguided "Ghost Busters"

Perry DeAngelis and Steven Novella

In 1996, Perry DeAngelis, a real estate manager, and Steven Novella, an assistant professor of neurology at the Yale School of Medicine, started the New England Skeptical Society so that New Englanders interested in the paranormal would have a forum for considering topics such as ghosts in a rational and scientific manner. The founders also hoped to counteract what they felt was the media's unquestioning treatment of these controversial topics. DeAngelis and Novella lived near a well-known ghost-hunting couple, Ed and Lorraine Warren, who claimed to have encountered ghosts and other paranormal entities many times over the past several decades.

DeAngelis and Novella paid a visit to the Warrens to investigate their claims and examine their evidence for the

From "Hunting the Ghost Hunters," by Perry DeAngelis and Steven Novella, *The Connecticut Skeptic*, Summer 1997. Copyright © 1997 by *The Connecticut Skeptic*. Reprinted with permission.

paranormal. They found that the Warrens, like many other people who claim to be ghost hunters, had no convincing evidence. The following selection describes their encounter with the Warrens.

Ed and Lorraine Warren have been investigating hauntings for over 40 years and claim to have mountains of proof for the existence of ghosts. We sought to examine their evidence to see if it stands up to the scientific rigor they claim to endorse.

Ed and Lorraine Warren hunt ghosts—ghosts, apparitions, demons, possessed people, places and things. They have been doing so for decades, and claim to have looked at nearly 8000 cases. They are world renowned for this practice, and they dwell right here in Monroe, Connecticut.

As a regional skeptical organization, we have taken on the task of investigating local paranormal claims. We sought to evaluate the phenomenon of ghosts (in the generic sense, referring to all manner of spiritual manifestations) and see if there is any evidence to support the hypothesis that the phenomenon exists. On the matter of hauntings, the Warrens are one of the preeminent experts, and they are local, so naturally we decided to look into their work. Also, they claim to have scientific evidence which does indeed prove the existence of ghosts, which sounds like a testable claim into which we can sink our investigative teeth. What we found was a very nice couple, some genuinely sincere people, but absolutely no compelling evidence, or, more precisely, there was a ton of "evidence," but none of it stands up to rigorous scientific testing, and most of it not even to cursory testing. None of it.

Like all pseudosciences, the field of ghost hunting makes

bold pretense to being legitimate science. The Warrens call their organization the New England Society for Psychic Research (NESPR), but as we will see, they are a "research" organization in name only. Their website proudly proclaims that "Our mission is to move the area of psychic phenomena out of the dark ages into the mainstream of rigorous scientific thought and inquiry." Yet upon inspection, their methods lack the components of genuine scientific inquiry or even the most fundamental attempt at scientific rigor. Rather than an earnest search for the truth, regardless of what that may be, their society seeks only to support their a priori assumption that the phenomenon is real.

Our investigation began with a tour through the Warrens' rather unique museum, housed in their basement, and alleged to be the most haunted place in Connecticut. Shortly after meeting Ed and Lorraine, two things became very clear to us. One, that they are sincere. They believe the things they say. And two, that they have precious little evidence to support their beliefs. What they do have in abundance, are ghost stories. During that first visit, and in the five hour interview that followed, we were treated to scores of Warren stories. However, despite their insistence to the contrary, stories are not evidence.

The Warrens

On the museum tour, Ed warned us not to touch anything in the main room, as we would open ourselves up to possible possession. If we did accidentally rub against something (which was nearly unavoidable in that crammed space), we were to report it, so that he could purify our auras before we left. The room was a clutter of collected stuff garnered over the Warrens' forty year career. This included paintings, masks, statuettes, and many books. One of these ghostly tomes was an "Unearthed Arcana," a Dungeons and Dragons role-playing game book. I still have a copy collecting dust in my closet. Ed claimed that the most dangerous item in the house, however, was a Raggedy-Ann doll that was said to still be possessed by a demonic entity. He keeps this enclosed in a glass case for safety, and chillingly relates the tale of the man who ignored his warnings and taunted the doll, only to die hours later in a tragic motorcycle accident.

Born in 1926, Ed Warren has been involved with the ghostly world since the age of five when he saw the apparition of a recently deceased landlady. Ed's father was a Connecticut State Trooper who went to mass every day. His grandfather was also very pious, and bequeathed the bulk of his estate to the Catholic church for the purchase of a stained glass window. It is not difficult to see the basis of Ed's belief structure, being reared in such a devout environment. The Catholic church does hold that supernatural entities can and do interact with the physical world. Ed also refers to NESPR as a theological institute, and states that his investigations are intimately associated with his religious convictions. In fact, one of his first questions to us, just as with other skeptics he has confronted in the past, is whether or not we believe in god, for without faith we could not understand his research.

Lorraine, born in 1927, is said to be a "sensitive," or clairvoyant. This is a person that can feel things psychically. When the Warrens go into an alleged haunted dwelling for the first time, three sensitives are utilized. If all three come up with positive "readings," or feelings, it is said to be powerful evidence of a supernatural presence. Of course, using an unproven method to measure an unproven phenomenon is of little scientific value.

As our probing into the Warrens' evidence continued, proceeding next into a prolonged interview, we asked to examine their most impressive or most convincing evidence, a request that we would repeat many times. But first, we needed to learn some of the jargon that is associated with the ghost phenomenon. Ed was kind enough to give us a crash course.

The "psychic" hours, Ed told us, are from 9 PM to 6 AM and the most vicious hauntings occur around 3 AM. Why? Because that is an insult to the Holy Trinity. A "ghost" is a luminescence without definable form, but on the other hand, an "apparition" has form and features. There are human spirits, and then there are the real bad guys, inhuman spirits. These are, of course, the essences of things never alive, or demonic entities. Ed also gave us some tips: always keep a vile of blessed water on your person to compel entities; if a possessed person meets your gaze, never be the first to break it, as that demonstrates weakness. And on it went, rules and jargon of the trade.

The Photographic Evidence

The vast majority of the Warrens' physical evidence is photographs. They have hundreds of ghost shots, taken by them and those who work for them. The Carousel Restaurant, location for the Warrens' weekly classes and said to be haunted, have their own collection of such photographs. Other ghost hunting societies, such as the Cosmic Society, another local group comprised of defectors from NESPR, also have a collection of such photos as their primary claim to evidence. Yet quantity is not a substitute for quality.

The bulk of these photos are simply blobs of light on a piece of film. There are dozens of ways to get such light artifacts onto film, but most fit into one of three categories: flashback, light defraction, or camera cords. Rare double or multiple exposures create more interesting, but still artifactual, photographs. It is significant to note that in almost every occurrence of a ghost photograph, the ghost is not seen at the time the photo is taken. It is not until the picture is developed that the ghost or glob or rod is seen, a strong indication that the picture is a result of photographic artifact.

Flashback is simply light from the camera flash reflected back at the lens, causing a hazy overexposed region on the film. The result is often a whispy and blurry light image on the film. It is easy to tell when a flash was used, because of the sharp shadows that are created and because objects in the foreground are brightly lit. The Warrens' website even suggests that using a flash will help create ghost photographs, and the brighter the flash the better. The website even admits that this flash effect is paradoxical, and was not expected, since they claim that such ghostly images are often psychically placed on the film by the spirits. However, there is no discussion or any recognition at all that the light images might be the result of photographic artifact created by the flash.

So-called "ghost globules" are spheres of light, rather than whispy forms. The images, however, are curiously reminiscent of light defracting around a point source. A small amount of condensation on the camera lens is enough to mass produce such ghost globules. Under the right conditions, any discrete source of light can produce this effect.

Paranormal investigator for CSICOP [Committee for the Scientific Investigation of Claims of the Paranormal] Joe Nickell made a valuable contribution to the field of photographic artifact when he discovered, through experimentation and common sense, the camera cord effect. The cord or strap of a camera can easily fall in front of the lens, and go unnoticed with cameras that do not view through the lens but through a separate aperture. Even black cords will look like white blobs or streaks of light (called "light rods") when they reflect the light of a flash. We were able to reproduce this effect on our first try, creating a "ghost" photograph as good as any we have seen.

Copious examples of all three of these common artifacts can be seen on the websites of the Warrens, the Cosmic Society, and other similar sites. What is lacking in all of them, however, is any consideration of alternate explanations of the photographs other than genuine ghosts. There is no investigation into natural sources for the blobs of light, no discussion of alternatives, no discussion at all, in fact. There is only the simple and unquestioned pronouncement that such blobs of light are evidence of the paranormal.

Video Evidence

The other evidence that the Warrens possess is video. Their piece-de-resistance is Ed's video of the famous White Lady of Union Cemetery, in Easton, Connecticut. We have only been able to view this tape in the Warrens' home because Ed refused to give it to us for analysis, a common theme in our investigation. The tape apparently shows a white human figure moving behind some tomb stones. Like videos of UFOs, Bigfoot, and the Loch Ness monster, however, the figure is at that perfect distance and resolution so that a provocative shape can be seen, but no details which would aid definitive identification. Ed Warren has not investigated the video with any scientific rigor, and refuses to allow others to do so. Despite Ed's insistence that he is engaged in scientific research, he continues to jealously horde his alleged evidence, rather than allowing it to be critically analyzed, as is necessary in genuine scientific endeavors.

The Warrens did, however, give us one of their other pieces of video evidence. This showed a man "dematerializing." It was taken by a mounted camera in a dining room in the middle of the night during one of their investigations. On the tape, a young man walks into the room, scratches his head, and "Poof!" disappears. This extraordinary occurrence is quickly followed by a "ghost light" appearing momentarily on the window behind the scene.

We gladly accepted the tape and took it to the HB Group, a professional video company, for detailed video analysis. An excerpt from that analysis is below:

> We are witnessing a wipe in this segment of videotape. Although there are several different ways in video editing to achieve a wiping effect, the most simple of ways has been employed here. Deliberately or accidentally, the camcorder stopped recording on the final frame of the person in the room and resumed recording just a few seconds after the person had moved outside of the view of the camera. On a related observation, the properties of light alone could dictate a hundred different explanations for the mysterious "dot" of light that appears a few seconds after the man "vanishes." However, I believe that this dot of light was caused by the reflection through the dining room window of the headlights of a passing car. The passing headlights can be seen if you watch the right hand side of the screen just after the "dot" of light fades out.

As you can see, the only piece of evidence that we were given turned out to be less than compelling. It was, in fact, a simple malfunction at best, and fraud at worst. Even cursory analysis of this piece of tape would have revealed what we found to the Warrens. Yet no one in the Warrens' investigatory network bothered to check it out. Rather than take this obvious first step, one of their investigators simply declared that the "ghost light" (the car headlights mentioned above) was "unexplainable." Further, none of the people in the tape were aware that anything had even occurred until the following day when the tape was viewed (again, the fingerprint of artifact), including the young man who allegedly dematerialized! Ed put his credibility in serious jeopardy when he looked at that tape, and without any verification, stated that experts, ". . . can only come to one conclusion, that kid disappeared."

Despite numerous attempts to examine other physical evidence the Warrens claim to possess, we were given nothing else. Instead, we were given excuses such as "The film was erased," "The people in the film want privacy," "We had just turned off the recording equipment, when . . ." Forty years of "research" into a phenomenon and precious little to show for it.

Eyewitness Testimony

Vastly outnumbering the Warrens' low grade physical evidence is their copious anecdotal evidence. They are great tellers of ghost stories, leading, in no small measure, to their popularity on the lecture circuit. They do not seem to understand, however, that the case for the reality of ghosts will never be made by stories alone.

In this respect, however, the Warrens are typical of the majority of people, who are compelled by a gripping story and lack a deep understanding of how flimsy and unreliable human memory and perception really is. Good skeptics, like good scientists, strive to increase their awareness of such weaknesses, so that they can be controlled for in the quest for knowledge. Ed and his ilk, on the other hand, are continuously seeking the "reliable witness." But even pilots, firefighters, police chiefs, and physicians, however, are just people. Their gray matter is the same as everyone else's.

In short, memory is fallible. This is due to the fact that all of our perceptions are filtered through our own unique polyglot of prejudices, preconceptions, misconceptions, insecurities and physical frailties. The mind can dilute, mix up, and even manufacture memories. And we have no way to determine which are which. Without external verification, there is no way to distinguish a delusion from a hallucination from a vivid dream from a genuine experience.

Further, many sightings or interactions with an entity

(whether ghost or alien) take place in the bedroom, late at night, or very early in the morning—times and places connected with sleep, or, more accurately, the near-sleep state. A classic example is Jack Smurl, investigated by the Warrens themselves, who related the tale of awakening in the early morning, being paralyzed, sensing an entity in the room, being overcome with terror, then being raped by a ghost. There is a well described neurological phenomenon known as hypnagogia. This occurs when we are between the waking and sleeping states, semi-conscious, and not fully aware. It is during these times that many alleged paranormal experiences manifest. Many believe that they are being abducted by aliens from their beds, others, like Jack Smurl, that they are visited by ghosts. During REM sleep, and continuing into waking dreams, our brain turns off the neurons that connect to our spinal column in order to keep us from acting out our dreams, and resulting in the sensation of paralysis during hypnagogia.

When we offered this to Ed as a possible alternate explanation, he seemed intrigued. "But," he continued confidently, "What about the pressure on the victim's chest when the entity is trying to get into them . . .?" Well, we were sorry to tell Ed that pressure on the chest and shortness of breath is also a well described aspect of hypnagogia.

"Oh," said Ed.

Sleep Deprivation and Fantasy

Many investigations of haunted houses take place into the wee hours of the night, forcing the investigators to stay up all night and creating sleep deprivation. In the sleep deprived state our brains are highly susceptible to hallucinations, and here is yet another fertile source of ghostly experiences.

Another prolific source is the human imagination. Different people have different capacities for imagination and fantasy. At the far end of the spectrum are individuals who are particularly prone to fantasy. Coupled with a desire to believe and immersion into a belief system with group support, such fantasy prone people can generate a tremendous amount of alleged paranormal experiences.

There is good reason to believe that groups such as NESPR would attract such individuals. With the Warrens' widespread exposure, there is ample opportunity to inadvertently "screen" many individuals. Hundreds or thousands will see one of their lectures in a year. Out of those, dozens will make the effort to go to one of their weekly classes. The ones that stay on for the long haul are invited on investigations. And among those, a few are deemed to be "sensitive," which means that they can see things that other people cannot.

Now, we do not expect everybody to be versed in hypnagogia, the effects of sleep deprivation, and the vagaries of the human imagination, but we do expect it from someone who claims to be conducting scientific research in a field where such phenomena play an important role. Ed Warren, however, had clearly not heard of hypnagogia prior to his association with us. Although he claims that his critics are closed-minded, he himself dismisses out-of-hand any alternative explanation of his evidence to the paranormal hypothesis, without investigation designed to do so. What passes for research in NESPR, and the field of ghost hunting in general, is passive documentation of anecdote and summary paranormal interpretation.

What Harm?

As skeptics, we are often asked, "What harm does belief in the paranormal do?" To this question, there is a very serious reply. To foster the air of gullibility that our society is awash in today is toxic, financially, emotionally, and sometimes terminally so. One need only look back several months to the 39 people snuffed out in an insane attempt to ride a UFO [in San Diego, California, members of a cult committed suicide en masse, believing they were meeting a UFO] for a vivid example. In the case of the Warrens, aside from adding to this aura of gullibility in general, they recount a case that brings the danger into sharp focus.

In July of 1996, the Warrens were contacted by a family in Westport, claiming to have a young girl who was possessed. They went to the home, with some new investigators, and took in the scene of an adolescent girl surrounded by her extended family, obviously in some kind of distress. In their desperation, however, the parents had also taken their child to a psychiatrist at Yale, who insisted that the Warrens not be involved in their child's case. Thankfully, the parents followed his advice, and the Warrens withdrew.

Yet what if the parents had not followed the physician's advice? The Warrens, who were feeding this poor girl's delusions, would have likely driven her deeper into madness. I do not believe that Ed or Lorraine would ever intentionally hurt a child, or anyone for that matter. Yet, their organization and activities lend a false legitimacy to the field of ghost hunting. Their claims reinforce delusions, have served as decisive court testimony, and confuse the public about the methods of legitimate science. To me, this case is what should stop one from smiling pleasantly at the funny ghost busting couple, and pause to take them very seriously indeed.

In the final analysis, the field of research into spiritual and ghostly phenomena lacks any scientific rigor. The field is fully and unreservedly a pseudoscience. The Warrens and their colleagues pay lip service to scientific principles, but when confronted with the lack of scientific quality to their methods and evidence they typically retreat, as Ed Warren did, to the position that "you can't have scientific evidence for a spiritual phenomenon." They want the respectability of science without the tedious work, careful thought, and high standards of evidence that it demands.

The Warrens and their society refused to allow the CSS to observe their investigatory techniques and refused to allow their "best" evidence to be examined. They are concerned about protecting their organization and the beliefs they represent, rather than the scientific search for truth, wherever it may lead—and that is what constitutes the gulf between skeptics and believers.

Ghosts Are Hallucinations

Michael White

A 2001 Gallup poll reported that one-third of all Americans believe they have seen a ghost. Is there an explanation for such sightings? Michael White, the author of the following selection, says that many researchers believe the explanation is simple: People who say they see ghosts are simply hallucinating. White explains several types of hallucinations that can cause a person (or even several people at a time) to believe they have seen a ghost. White is a former director of scientific studies at d'Overbroeck's College in Oxford, England, and the science editor of British *GQ* magazine. He has also written several books on scientific topics and was a consultant for the Discovery Channel's series *The Science of the Impossible*.

The most interesting of all so-called *trivial* explanations for ghosts is hallucination, and many researchers—both en-

Excerpted from *Weird Science: An Expert Explains Ghosts, Voodoo, the UFO Conspiracy, and Other Paranormal Phenomena,* by Michael White (New York: Avon Books, 1999). Copyright © 1999 by Michael White. Reprinted with permission.

thusiasts of the occult and empirically minded skeptics—accept that the vast majority of apparitions can be explained in this way.

Hallucination is an intensely researched psychological state that is surprisingly widespread. Back at the turn of the nineteenth century one of the most useful pieces of data gathered by the SPR [Society for Psychical Research] was a survey conducted on 17,000 people to determine the incidence of hallucination. They found that 2,300 of those asked had experienced a hallucination sometime during their lives, and according to a modern-day survey of American college students, seventy percent claimed they had experienced the auditory hallucination of hearing voices while awake.

In his book, *Fire in the Mind*, the psychologist Ronald K. Siegel has said of hallucinations:

> In the past, hallucinations were often regarded as the exclusive domain of the insane. Through the research and cases in this book, we begin to understand that anyone can have them. They arise from common structures in the brain and nervous system, common biological experiences, and common reactions of the brain to stimulation or deprivation. The resultant images may be bizarre, but they are not necessarily crazy. They are simply based on stored images in our brains. Like a mirage that shows a magnificent city on a desolate expanse of ocean or desert, the images of hallucinations are actually reflected images of real objects located elsewhere.

Hypnagogic and Hypnopompic Hallucinations

The most common time to see a ghost is late at night and usually at the point of going to sleep. The "ghost at the end of the bed" is the stuff of legend and the mainstay of horror films, yet there is a well-understood reason for this. As the body switches from the voluntary nervous system—the system that allows us to function in our everyday lives—to the involuntary nervous system, we commonly experience what are called *hypnagogic hallucinations*. One interpretation of these is that "our wires get crossed," the brain is momentarily confused by the switch from one nervous system to the other, and images are dredged up from either deep in the conscious memory or from the subconscious. This, it is believed, accounts for the vast majority of apparitions.

These visions or hallucinations can seem very real and may be accompanied by auditory sensations or even smells. A similar experience is sleepwalking. Many people have at one time or another had the odd experience of suddenly coming to in the bathroom or sitting in front of a blank television screen in the den. Often these experiences seem very real at the time but are almost totally forgotten by the following morning.

Another common form of sleep-related hallucination is what has been dubbed *hypnopompic hallucination* and occurs when we awaken. Again, this is due to the body switching nervous systems, this time from the involuntary to the voluntary, and may account for a large number of cases of apparition.

Both hypnagogic and hypnopompic hallucination may also be used to explain what have become known as "hitchhiker apparitions." Since the beginning of the car age, an increasingly common phenomenon within ghost mythology describes accounts of drivers seeing ghostly figures in or at the side of the road. These sightings often occur along stretches of road famous for particularly grizzly accidents or known in the region for apparent spectral activity. Sometimes drivers have even reported knocking down people, feeling the bump of the body under the car, and when they have gone to see what had happened, they're left staring at empty pavement.

Even more dramatic incidents tell of drivers tending someone they believed they had hit, covering them with a blanket, only to find the body had vanished by the time the police arrived. In 1979 a driver named Roy Fulton claimed he picked up a male hitchhiker along a stretch of road in Stanbridge, Bedfordshire, late at night. The young man opened the door and sat silently on the backseat, ignoring Fulton's attempts to begin a conversation. Only when Fulton turned to offer the hitchhiker a cigarette did he realize the boy had vanished.

Such incidents are open to ridicule and to claims of hoaxing, and perhaps a large proportion of them are deliberate frauds, but in some cases they could be put down to either hypnagogic or hypnopompic hallucination. Drivers sometimes fall asleep at the wheel, and it is quite possible hallucinations could occur as they lose consciousness or wake suddenly. These brain-generated visions are then amplified by environmental effects and individual circumstances. Driving alone along narrow country roads in the dark can induce suggestive images in the mind, and speeding along a seemingly endless stretch of featureless highway is often almost mesmerizing.

Crisis Apparitions

A related phenomenon is crisis apparition, where sighters sense the presence of someone they know either close to or at the point of death. There are many documented cases in which people have apparently seen projections of close relatives or friends who were in a crisis situation at the time, often immediately before their moment of death. In their book *Phantasms of the Living*, Edmund Gurney, Frederick Myers, and Frank Podmore documented 701 cases of apparent crisis projection and admitted they could not explain many of these incidents.

One of the most famous stories of crisis apparition comes from the 1930s. One stormy, freezing night in the mid-Atlantic, a one-eyed English pilot named Hinchliffe with his female copilot was attempting the first east-west crossing of the ocean when suddenly their biplane hit bad weather. The high winds tossed it around, the compass was disturbed by magnetic interference, and without a reference point for hundreds of miles in any direction they were soon hopelessly lost. The plane began to nose-dive toward the waves, its engine screaming in protest, and a moment later it hit the water, killing pilot and copilot instantly.

The same night, two friends of Hinchliffe's, Squadron Leader Rivers Oldmeadow and Colonel Henderson, were steaming toward New York aboard an ocean liner several hundred miles away from the scene of the crash. Neither of them had seen Hinchliffe for some time and they were totally unaware he and his female colleague had attempted the flight. It was in the middle of the night, just when, according to later corroboration, Hinchliffe's plane hit the storm, that Colonel Henderson, dressed in his pajamas, burst into his friend's room shouting:

> God, Rivers, something ghastly has happened. Hinch has just been in my cabin. Eyepatch and all. It was ghastly. He kept repeating over and over again, "Hendy, what am I going to do? What am I going to do? I've got the woman with me and I'm lost. I'm lost." Then he disappeared in front of my eyes. Just disappeared.

Supporters of paranormal explanations for ghosts and apparitions have proposed that this incident and others like it are due to a form of emergency or crisis telepathy, that at the moment of death the human brain is capable of transmitting an image or news of a person's situation, perhaps as a final survival attempt. But it is also possible to see such events in a far more prosaic light.

Simpler Explanations

First, there is the strong possibility of hallucination. The sighter in this story, Colonel Henderson, may well have enjoyed a pleasant evening at the captain's table before turning in for the night, and could have experienced an alcohol-induced hypnagogic hallucination.

But, say the enthusiasts, how does this account for the fact that Henderson had no idea his friend was in the middle of a risky flight?

The answer is, he almost certainly did know about it subconsciously. It is possible he had been reading a newspaper and noted subliminally an article about his friend attempting an Atlantic crossing without reading the piece or even realizing consciously that he had spotted it. This could then have enhanced his hallucination, providing the subconscious image around which he produced the vision.

An alternative suggestion for this and many other cases of crisis apparition is that people have a subconscious knowledge of an event but need to create an hallucination in order to process the information through their conscious mind. The usual reasons for this inhibition are fear and guilt. These emotions could force the conscious mind away from analyzing or thinking about a situation, and the brain then has to resort to filtering the information through an alternative system where it does not meet the same resistance.

A final explanation for hallucinations appearing as crisis apparitions is wishful thinking or comfort thinking. When this is the source, the visions are called *need-based hallucinations*.

Most people hope there is an afterlife, and many, especially those who feel insecure or fearful, can experience this desire so strongly they produce "evidence" to support their wishes. To them, a ghost is proof of an afterlife, and so their subconscious mind is empowered to conjure up an appro-

priate image. In other situations people can imagine they
are being visited by a comforting, supportive figure who either warns them of imminent danger or gives them extra
impetus to fulfill a difficult task. The record-breaking driver,
Donald Campbell, claimed he'd been visited by his father
Sir Malcolm Campbell on many occasions, and believed his
father had been sent to warn him of impending danger.

Hauntings and Poltergeists

Of a quite different order to apparitions is the phenomenon
of haunting, especially poltergeist activity. Hauntings are
usually witnessed by several people and encompass a wide
range of apparently supernatural activities—materializing
and dematerializing of objects, noises, smells, and, on rare
occasions, violent, even life-threatening incidents.

When a group of people all witness the same set of experiences, it is very difficult to explain them as hallucination, hoax, or any other natural process. But many do yield
to rather mundane causes if the investigators probe deeply
enough.

The first stage in any investigation of a haunting is to
eliminate natural sounds and smells. These may take some
searching, and enthusiasts of occult explanations are fond
of listing cases in which months of investigation into particular hauntings have been wasted and no link to natural
causes detected. These cases are rare and do not offer proof
of supernatural activity, they simply show the researchers
did not investigate thoroughly enough.

After hoaxes, natural causes, and illusions have been
ruled out, we can again turn to hallucination. Surprising as
it may seem, it is possible for a group of individuals to experience the same reduced images. This phenomenon is
called *mass hallucination*, and is brought about when one of
the group is a stronger personality than the others and cre-

ates a convincing suggestion which is then adopted by the others. This explains many cases of hauntings involving parents and children where one of the adults—or in rare cases, one of the children—unwittingly implants the idea, after which fear and anxiety take over.

Infectious Hallucinations

Enthusiasts of the occult take this idea and add an element of the supernatural to create what they call the *infectious hallucination theory*. This proposes that one of the group experiences an hallucination which is then transmitted telepathically to the others. But psychologists have shown through experiment that this mechanism is actually quite unnecessary. If the correct blend of personalities are put together in an atmosphere of perceived danger and fear, an hallucination created by one of the stronger personalities is infectious enough to spread to the others without the need for telepathy.

The final explanation for poltergeists, and one supported by some enthusiasts of the occult, is the idea that emotional disturbance in human beings can be projected into dramatic physical events. The theory suggests that people with the ability to project telepathic images may, if they are placed in an emotionally challenging situation, produce enough psychic energy to move furniture or throw objects across a room.

The energy needed to do this is of a quite different order to that generated by the human brain, and, according to the known laws of physics, is completely impossible. A less problematic explanation may be that a human source of hallucination is planting images into the minds of the witnesses. Again there is no need for telepathy in this situation. If the creator of the image is a strong enough character, they may be able to induce hallucinations in the other witnesses. They may even be able to convince those on the receiving end of any violent activity that they actually feel pain or have cuts, burns, and bruises.

Poltergeist activity has been shown to center around children and teenagers more frequently than adults; in particular, pubescent girls appear to be a common source. This has led occultists to the idea that hormonal and emotion imbalance enhances PK [psychokinesis] abilities in these young women. A more logical explanation might be that during a time in which body and brain chemistry is in a disturbed state, the subjects could be capable of encouraging hallucinations in those around them by suggestion and emotional manipulation. Mothers placed in highly stressful situations, thanks to the growing pains of their teenage girls, might be particularly susceptible, especially if the notion their home is haunted has already been "seeded" in their minds.

Ghostly Explanations

Joe Nickell

Ghost accounts share many common elements, from mysterious lights to strange sounds. But are such phenomena really without explanation? Not according to Joe Nickell. In the following selection, Nickell reviews several themes common to ghostly occurrences and suggests more ordinary explanations for them. Nickell has been a stage magician, private investigator, and technical writing teacher. He has also written several books on mysterious topics and frequently conducts investigations for the Committee for the Scientific Investigation of Claims of the Paranormal.

Whether they are the result of imagination or of other causes, ghostly phenomena are often related in terms of particularly striking *motifs* (or story elements). Some may involve illusions of various kinds, even outright hoaxes. Of course these may be augmented by individual or collective

Excerpted from *Entities: Angels, Spirits, Demons, and Other Alien Beings*, by Joe Nickell (Amherst, NY: Prometheus Books, 1995). Copyright © 1995 by Joe Nickell. Reprinted by permission of the publisher.

belief to produce vivid spectral phenomena. Motifs discussed here include the ghost at the bedside, strange specters, phantom footfalls, haunted rocking chair, ghostly door, light in the window, "spook lights," phantom hitchhiker, and other motifs.

Ghost at the Bedside

. . . [Psychology professor] Dr. Robert A. Baker states:

> People are easily haunted especially at night after retiring. One of the most common experiences occurs in the middle of the night when the sleeping person suddenly awakes and finds to his astonishment a ghostly figure standing by his or her bed. On many occasions this figure may be a vision of someone near and dear who has just died, or it may well be a vision of a monster or a demon or an alien spaceman. The person experiencing the vision is also startled to discover he is paralyzed, unable to move, and often experiences a floating sensation of moving across the room, out the door, through the walls, etc. Accompanying this experience is a feeling of calm and detachment as if the experience is happening to someone else. After the vision disappears or the experience is over, the percipient usually calmly goes back to sleep as if nothing happened.

. . . Such a vision is termed a "waking dream."

Such a dream and the power of suggestion may combine to create a ghost tradition in an ancestral home. There are many reported family legends relating to a haunted bed, for example, that of North Hill House in Colchester, England, described by Dr. Nandor Fodor [a psychoanalyst and psychic researcher]. Supposedly the ghost haunted a large double bed in the house, "a glum-looking, rickety place." Some people only vaguely felt an air of depression in the room while others reported dreams of strangulation. Fodor amusingly relates his own experience at North Hill House—due apparently to the effect of the spooky environs and his own heightened expectations:

I hoped that the strangler would pay me a visit while I was sleeping in the haunted bed. I fixed up a stereo camera on a tripod, covering the bed and the corner of a powder closet which was said to be the center of the disturbance. I used flash bulbs and infrared plates. The camera cord reached to my bed and I opened the camera after the light was put out.

It was a glorious bed. I never felt so comfortable in all my life. In no time I was in sound sleep.

I dreamed that the ghost, with a black doctor's bag and a very professional look, came to cure me of insomnia. He made passes over my head and when I refused to yield, he shook his head disapprovingly: "You are too tough, a radical cure is necessary. I regret to have to strangle you."

As he threw himself on me, I awoke gasping. My hand tightened on the flash bulb lead. There was a blinding flare which must have frightened the ghost, if he was there, for the photograph showed no one but myself.

I investigated a somewhat similar tradition at Liberty Hall in Frankfort, Kentucky, a historical site and the residence, supposedly, of an ethereal "Lady in Gray." The ghost is said to be that of a woman, an aunt of the original mistress of the house, who died in 1817. One source, citing "a very interesting tradition handed down in the family," asserts she died in an upstairs bedroom that is now called the "Ghost Room."

Interestingly, there is no recorded mention of the ghost from the time of the aunt's death until at least sixty-five years later. Only one source describes the supposed first visitation of the ghost—i.e., the "origination of the expression 'Ghost Room.'" According to this source, Miss Mary Mason Scott, great-grand-daughter of the original owners, was at the time "home from finishing school" and occupied the room in which her early relative had died. Then, "in the dead of night," she "ran screaming from the room exclaiming that she had seen a ghost"—a "Lady in Gray" as she described the apparition. Thus it appears that the ghostly tradition was launched by an impressionable and apparently quite emotional schoolgirl (who remained unmarried until her death in 1934 and who dabbled in fortunetelling and similar occult pursuits).

Since the sighting occurred when the young lady was abed, there is every likelihood that she experienced an ordinary waking dream of the ghost-at-the-bedside variety. As to her reaction, [history professor] R.C. Finucane writes of the Victorians that "some percipients became hysterical, others turned over and went back to sleep; both men and women ran the entire gamut of emotional responses." As described, the ghost was just the type of image a young Victorian lady would have conjured up, since ethereal gray ladies represented the typical fashion in ghosts during Victoria's reign.

Strange Specters

Many people see ghosts while fully awake and in bright light. One example comes from a small frame house in Lexington, Kentucky. Among other occurrences, when the mother was in her bedroom sewing, she would see a ghostly flash of white pass by her door. Investigation by Dr. Baker revealed: "When lights were on in the bath or the headlights from a passing car shown in the bathroom window, they were reflected off the mirror in the door, and when the door moved it was as if someone had flashed a searchlight across the bedroom door."

Similarly, [magician] Milbourne Christopher explains how "a billowing curtain becomes a shrouded woman" and "a shadow becomes a menacing intruder to those with vivid imaginations." Reflections, the misperception of movement seen out of the corner of the eye (a common illusion), and other effects of light and shadow can give rise to specters.

An interesting case I investigated was that of the supposedly haunted La Fonda Inn in Santa Fe. At least one man lost his life there in 1857 when he was lynched in the hotel's back yard. Reports of other hangings and shootings are part of the local tradition, as are stories of ghosts that supposedly roam the grounds. When I interviewed several of the inn's employees in late May of 1993, I found that while most had heard of the ghost and some knew of secondhand reports, almost no one had seen anything out of the ordinary. This was especially significant in the case of one man, who had been a bell captain there for forty-three years yet had never had any ghostly experiences.

A young female employee did say she had once seen an apparition, a ghostly figure in a white gown carrying a bouquet. This was supposedly the traditional ghost of a bride killed on her honeymoon (although one wonders at the incongruity of what was presumably a bridal bouquet being carried on such an occasion). Under questioning, the employee stated that she did not believe in ghosts, and she soon said she was "not convinced" that what she actually saw was a ghost. She admitted that what she saw "could have been a reflection from the dining room"—one presumably that she colored with her own imagination.

I have done something of the sort. Some years ago while driving at night, I saw ahead of me a stooped old man standing by the roadside. A moment later, however, he had vanished Fortunately, I just had time to see that what had looked like an old man had really been only a stump and some leaves seen from a particular angle. As the angle changed abruptly the illusion was lost.

Phantom Footfalls

Another common motif is that of ghostly footfalls heard in a house when there is no one present to cause them. These can be an illusion caused by any of a number of sources,

ranging from simply the odd noises produced by the set-
tling of an old house to fruit-laden branches bumping a
roof, or any of numerous other possibilities.

One interesting case that some friends told me about involved a staircase in an old house that had a loose tread covering the steps. As one walked up or down the stairs, each
depressed tread would pop back into place a moment later,
giving the eerie illusion that someone was following who-
ever was on the stairs.

The most interesting example of the mysterious footsteps
motif that I have investigated was at Mackenzie House [in
Toronto, Ontario]. In 1960 Mr. and Mrs. Alex Dobban, who
had succeeded the Edmundses as caretakers, told the *Toronto
Telegram* about certain ghostly events in the house, including mysterious footsteps on the stairs late at night. Mrs.
Dobban stated: "We hadn't been here long when I heard
footsteps going up the stairs. I called to my husband, but he
wasn't there. There was no one else in the house, but I definitely heard feet on the stairs." Subsequently Mrs. Edmunds
came forward to reinforce the claim. She stated that what
she had heard were "thumping footsteps like someone with
heavy boots," adding, "This happened frequently where
there was no one in the house but us, when we were sitting
together upstairs."

Some twelve years later, after the heavy-footed Mackenzie
ghost had been immortalized in further articles and books,
I investigated the site, learning almost immediately of a par-
allel staircase, made of iron, in a building next door, separated from Mackenzie House by only the narrowest of walk-
ways! That this was the source of the phantom footsteps was
corroborated by a tour guide in the historic house, who had
heard the sounds herself and managed once to reach the
stairs and hear the sounds coming from next door, and by
the building superintendent next door, who had known the

secret—obvious to him—for more than a decade. The latter said I was the first investigator to come next door, despite the proximity of the buildings. He had decided, bemusedly, to say nothing until asked. It had taken a dozen years.

Haunted Rocking Chair

This is yet another extremely common motif. At Liberty Hall, for instance, a rocker was occasionally seen "going back and forth by itself." There are several possible explanations for such an event, including drafts. Milbourne Christopher states: "The strangest air-induced action I have seen was when a child's rocking chair moved back and forth by itself, until the slightly opened window directly behind it was closed. The chair was on an uncarpeted floor, and there was a heavy wind at the time."

At one haunted historic house I saw an empty rocker move and was momentarily startled. Then I realized that a tour guide who had just walked by the chair without seeming to touch it had actually whacked it inadvertently with the hoop of her antebellum skirt.

One haunted rocker case I personally investigated was that of the historic Brown-Pusey House in Elizabethtown, Kentucky. Although I had heard the claim of the rocker's movement from a credible local source, to my surprise the house's long-time receptionist assured me it was news to her. In fact, she noted that her desk was immediately below the room where the rocker had been situated and that she would surely have heard it had it been active. The rocker was no longer in that room, but when I entered the chamber I immediately perceived the probable cause of the reported event: the floor was so rickety that walking on it caused even a dresser mirror to shake noticeably.

There are other possible explanations for "haunted" rockers including deliberate pranks, a resident house cat or other pet, an overactive imagination, and other potential sources of "ghostly" activity.

Ghostly Door

Like rocking chairs, doors may occasionally appear to move without human agency and be associated with ghosts. At the same time many of the forces that can animate a rocker—pets, rickety floors, pranksters, etc.—can also cause a door to move.

The recently retired curator of Liberty Hall, Mary Smith, told me of a rear door of the historic house that was usually kept ajar and that sometimes moved back and forth. However, unlike her predecessor who promoted the ghost as being good for business, Mrs. Smith is a skeptic who attributes the movement to the wind. During her tenure of more than fifteen years she did not experience any phenomena she attributed to the presence of a ghost.

Before Mrs. Smith's tenure, when ghost stories about the house were fostered and encouraged, once after a fire a fireman and newspaperman stayed in the building for three nights to prevent vandalism. They later told how doors shut behind them and candles were snuffed out "by sudden drafts of cool air." However, drafts are common to old houses—no doubt especially so after a fire—and, together with wind that has found its way through cracked panes, slightly open windows, and other sources, has been responsible for many ghostly occurrences. Obviously the same drafts that snuffed out the candles could be responsible for closing the doors.

In 1978 I investigated the quite sensational claims of a haunted door that graced an abandoned eastern Kentucky farmhouse. According to local tradition, a child was crushed to death in a cane mill accident nearby late in the [1800s]. The door was supposedly used to carry the child's mangled body which was later buried on a hill overlooking the farm. At the time of my investigation, the door was alleged to bang back and forth on occasion—or at least to produce such sounds. Workmen across the creek, who looked as the sounds continued briefly, were sure the door had not moved. A young hunter told me he had heard a banging sound "like someone stacking lumber" but checked and found no one there. Also, local residents told me, after a rain one could often see blood-like streaks running down the door!

Accompanied by the young hunter, my father and I visited the site. The house had been used in recent years as a makeshift barn for curing tobacco. Long two-by-four planks had been nailed up to serve as racks for hanging the tobacco. And a front room even had the side window enlarged into an open doorway for easy access. It was while we were standing in this room that the "ghost" manifested itself. Bam! Bam-bam-bam-bam. We looked at each other and the young man had a sheepish look. The door to the room, located immediately behind the "haunted" front door, had been opened against one of the two-by-fours, and a momentary gentle breeze had drifted up the branch, through the side opening, rattling the door against the plank. The gust spent, the noise ceased.

As our companion agreed, this noise would account for the sounds both he and the workmen had heard. Of course the *front* door had not moved at all, yet it had seemed the source of the noise. As to the "blood," it proved only to be dark streaks of water-borne substances, possibly tar, decaying leaves, dirt, etc., washing down from the roof. Later forensic tests proved no blood was present.

Light in the Window

This motif is widely reported, one instance being a mysterious light seen one evening by two security officers looking up at the third-story tower window of White Hall, the central Kentucky home of Cassius Marcellus Clay (1810–1903), the politician and abolitionist. Investigating, the officers found no one in the tower and were unable to explain the strange occurrence.

Such events, however, often turn out to be reflections from the moon or other light source on the window, an effect I have witnessed on more than one occasion. It can look exactly like a light *inside* the house. Milbourne Christopher relates the following interesting case study:

> Edward Saint, who was Mrs. Harry Houdini's manager during her last years in Hollywood, was intrigued by the tale that a specter had been observed moving from room to room in a deserted suburban house; the lantern it carried was visible through the windows. The ghost always walked one route from a room at the right end of the house to the left; it never went in the opposite direction. Saint discovered that the moving light so many people had reported was not in the house. It was the reflection from the headlights of an automobile as it approached the house. As a car came up the road the reflected beams went, as the car progressed, from window to window—the path the ghost always traveled.

"Spook Lights"

In many locales across the United States there are reports of "spook lights," ghostly illuminations that are steeped in folklore. Among the most famous of such phenomena is the intermittent Brown Mountain Light located in the western North Carolina mountains. As is the case with many such mysterious lights, the Brown Mountain phenomenon may have more than one cause. For example, in 1913 the United States Geological Survey investigated the light and concluded it was merely reflections of the head lamps of trains at the base of the mountain. However, since the phenomenon has been reported since 1771, other explanations have been proffered, including St. Elmo's Fire (a type of electrical discharge), so-called "earthquake lights" (an as yet little-understood phenomenon that is associated with seismic disturbances), and other possible sources. Less likely is the folkloric explanation that the light is the moon's reflection from a great gem located somewhere on the face of the mountain.

Another famous phenomenon of this type is that of the Marfa lights near Marfa, Texas. While not ruling out other possibilities, one investigation demonstrated that what are usually seen were automobile headlights merged into a single light due to the viewing distance of about thirty miles. Because of the distance, the light does not appear to be moving, but it does wink on and off as the car goes out of sight behind a cut or other obstruction.

More relevant to our discussion are ghost lights that appear over a graveyard just outside the town of Silver Cliff, Colorado. Again, various theories are offered, but some people insist that the phenomenon is merely the result of lights from nearby towns being reflected from tombstones.

A small hillside cemetery in eastern Kentucky is the source of another ghost light that supposedly shines from the grave of a nine-year-old girl. In fact, the light is a "rectangular halo around the front of the headstone" and is visible only from a particular spot on the bank of the nearby creek. These details suggest the light is a reflection and, indeed, the owner of a grocery near the spot believes the source may be a nearby security light. In any event, when crowds of up to two hundred sightseers continued to gather at the spot, the mother of the dead child abruptly covered the granite tombstone with a blanket. The light ceased.

Phantom Hitchhiker

In his book *The Encyclopedia of Ghosts*, Daniel Cohen terms this "unquestionably the most popular and widespread ghostly legend in the United States." Briefly stated, the typical version of the tale has a young man driving along a lonely road one rainy night when he stops for a hitchhiker, a teenage girl wearing a party dress. He gives the shivering girl his jacket, but when he arrives at her stated destination in the next city, she has disappeared! Knocking at the door, the young man learns she was killed ten years ago in an automobile accident on the very road where he encountered her. Later, when he looks for his jacket, it, too, has disappeared. Next day he locates the family plot in the cemetery, whereupon, neatly folded atop the girl's tombstone, is the missing jacket!

There are many versions of the proliferating legend, but no one appears to know just when and where it originated. For our purposes, perhaps, it is enough to know that it is a century-old tale that well illustrates the human desire for legend making, especially concerning the spine-tingling realm of the unrequited dead.

Other Motifs

The foregoing is only a beginning. Numerous other motifs in the form of mysterious sights and sounds could easily be given. However, perhaps those we have discussed thus far are sufficient to make clear the role the human imagination plays in cases of alleged haunting. As Dr. Baker says, "We tend to see and hear those things we believe in." The examples should also point to the necessity of investigating claims on a case-by-case basis and demonstrate a panoply of potential sources for many supposedly ghostly occurrences.

Epilogue: Analyzing the Evidence

"I see dead people." This is the most famous line in a suspense-filled 1999 movie called *The Sixth Sense*. The movie is about a young boy who sees ghosts and the psychologist who tries to help him cope with these visions. Ghosts are a popular topic for movies, and some people believe this is where ghosts belong—in a fictional world that no one takes too seriously. But others believe that ghosts are as real as their next-door neighbors. Which view is right?

When considering a controversial topic like ghosts and poltergeists, we must take care to look at the evidence available from more than one perspective. We can begin to shape our beliefs by critically examining the evidence provided by experts who have studied ghosts and those who claim to have experienced ghosts. Each article in this book provides various kinds of evidence and makes various kinds of arguments favoring or challenging the existence of ghosts and poltergeists. Some articles directly contradict others. It is the reader's job to decide which articles present a truthful and reasonable case for—or against—the existence of ghosts and poltergeists.

You can do this by reading each article critically. This does not mean criticizing, or saying negative things, about an article. It means analyzing and evaluating what the author says. This epilogue describes a critical reading technique and gives you practice using it to evaluate the articles in this book. You can use the same technique to evaluate information about other topics.

The Author

In deciding whether an article provides good evidence for or against the existence of ghosts, it can be helpful to find out something about the author. Consider whether the author has any special qualifications for writing about the subject. For example, in this book some authors claim to have experienced ghosts themselves. Others have taken a scientific approach to investigating ghost cases. Still others claim to be able to communicate with ghosts. You will have to decide what kind of experience makes an author more credible.

In this book, the editor has provided at least a small amount of information about each author. Use this information to start forming your opinion about the author's claims.

Hypothetical Reasoning

Despite whether you know anything about the author, you can evaluate an article on its own merits by using hypothetical reasoning. This is a method for determining whether something makes sense, whether an author has made a reasonable case for his or her claims. For example, Ed and Lorraine Warren, authors of the article "We Have Encountered Ghosts," claim that they have seen ghosts. You can use hypothetical reasoning to decide whether they have made a reasonable case supporting this claim. (Keep in mind that hypothetical reasoning will not necessarily prove that an author's claims are true—only that he or she has or has not made a reasonable case for the claims. By determining this, you know whether the arguments are worth considering when you are deciding whether ghosts are real.)

To use hypothetical reasoning to analyze an article, you will use five steps:

1. State the author's claim (the hypothesis).

2. Gather the author's evidence supporting the claim.
3. Examine the author's evidence.
4. Consider alternative hypotheses, or explanations, for the evidence.
5. Draw a conclusion about the author's claim.

Using hypothetical reasoning to examine several articles on ghosts and poltergeists can give you a better perspective on the topic. You will begin to discern the difference between strong and weak evidence and to see which point of view has the most—or the best—evidence supporting it.

In the following sections, we will use hypothetical reasoning to critically examine some of the articles in this book. You can practice applying the method to other articles.

1. State the Author's Claim (the Hypothesis)

A hypothesis is a factual statement that can be tested to determine the likelihood of its truth. In other words, it is not merely someone's opinion; by testing it we can determine if it is true or false. To evaluate an article critically, start by stating the author's claim. This will be the hypothesis you are going to test as you critically examine the article. The author may make several claims. To simplify, we will state one claim for each article.

Author	Hypothesis
Lance Morrow	Houses retain the spirits of those who have lived there.
Vincent H. Gaddis	There is a certain kind of poltergeist that starts fires.
Ed and Lorraine Warren	We have seen and communicated with ghosts.
Louis E. LaGrand	People often see the ghost of a departed loved one.
Joshua P. Warren	

Author	Hypothesis
Hilary Evans	
Bertram Rothschild	Ghosts are not real.
James Randi	The Columbus poltergeist was a fraud.
Perry DeAngelis and Steven Novella	Ed and Lorraine Warren don't have any evidence that ghosts are real.
Michael White	
Joe Nickell	

One important thing to remember when you write a hypothesis is that it should be a factual statement that is clear, specific, and provable. Look at the hypothesis for the Bertram Rothschild article as stated in the table above: "Ghosts are not real." This statement is very general and is difficult to prove or disprove. It is better to make the hypothesis more specific. The following hypothesis is more specific and, if the author does his job right, can be proven true or false.

Bertram Rothschild	People can easily fool themselves into believing they have seen a ghost.

Are there other hypotheses in the table above that should be more specific?

Note that not every article has a provable hypothesis. If an article is purely a writer's opinion, you may not be able to state a provable hypothesis. Likewise, some authors avoid stating any clear claim. For example, many newspaper and magazine articles attempt to remain as objective as possible about a topic. They simply report what happened and what people say about it. You may not be able to write a provable hypothesis for such an article.

In the table above, four hypothesis spaces have been left empty. Write a clear, specific, and provable hypothesis for each of these four articles.

2. Gather the Author's Evidence Supporting the Claim

Once you have a hypothesis, you must gather the evidence the author uses to support that hypothesis. The evidence is everything the author uses to prove that his or her claim is true. Sometimes an individual sentence is a piece of evidence. Sometimes a string of paragraphs or a section of the article is a piece of evidence. Let's look at the article by Louis E. LaGrand, "Ghosts Comfort the Living." Here is a partial list of LaGrand's evidence:

1. The author states that people of all ages have had contact experiences with deceased loved ones (ghosts).
2. The author states that ghosts have been part of the human experience throughout history.
3. The author states that a stigma is attached to reporting unsubstantial things like ghosts.
4. The author provides several eyewitness reports.
5. The author mentions the ghost experiences of some famous people—first lady Mary Todd Lincoln and psychologist Carl Jung.
6. The author tells us that Jung found a book exactly where he had seen it in a ghostly vision.

3. Examine the Evidence the Author Uses to Support the Claim

An author might use many types of evidence to support his or her claims. It is important to recognize different types of evidence and to evaluate whether they actually support the author's claims. LaGrand's main form of evidence is eyewitness testimony. He also uses statements of fact (items 1 and 2), implied logical reasoning (item 3), expert or celebrity testimonial (items 5 and 6), and physical evidence (item 6).

Eyewitness testimony. This brief article contains six vivid reports of people's encounters with deceased loved ones. To some people, these accounts alone would be enough to convince them that ghosts are real. But a scientist would examine these accounts carefully because eyewitness testimony is notoriously unreliable.

Perhaps you know about the eyewitness experiment in which a group of people is sitting in a classroom listening to a lecture or doing some other activity. Suddenly, the classroom door bursts open and a stranger enters. The stranger may "rob" one of the witnesses or do something else dramatic. Then the stranger leaves.

A few moments later, the instructor asks the students to tell what they witnessed. Invariably, different students remember different things. One remembers that the stranger was of average height and weight; another remembers that he was thin or heavy. One remembers that he had red hair; another remembers that a hood covered the stranger's head. One remembers that he was carrying a weapon; another remembers that his hands were empty. And so on.

When something unexpected happens, especially when it happens quickly or when it evinces great emotion, the mind is not prepared to remember details. Even when the event is expected, the witness can see things differently than what actually happened. This unreliability has many causes: Some people simply are not good observers. Others have preconceived ideas that influence their observation; for example, they may believe that all robbers are male, so when they see a robber whose features are not very clear, they assume the person must be male. Some people have recently experienced something that influences what they see. For instance, if you have just come home from a scary movie, hearing an unusual sound in your house can make you certain you are about to be set upon by a monster or a serial killer. In situations like the ones described in LaGrand's article, the grief the witnesses are experiencing may influence what they see—or even cause them to have a hallucination of a ghost, according to some experts.

For these reasons and more, you have to be very careful about accepting eyewitness testimony as the main kind of evidence. This is why in crime investigations, for example, the police often try to find independent corroborating witnesses—several people who saw the same event and have not spoken with each other so that their accounts have not been influenced by anyone else's version. If two or more witnesses independently report the same details, the chances are better that the details are accurate.

In LaGrand's article, there are no corroborating witnesses. This does not mean that the witnesses did not see what they claimed; it just means that we have to consider their testimony carefully and look for other kinds of evidence that may help support the eyewitness testimony.

Statements of fact (items 1 and 2). A statement of fact presents verifiable information—that is, it can be proven true (or false). Either the author verifies the information for us by providing the source of the information, or we can find out for ourselves. We can look up *ghosts* in an encyclopedia or on the Internet and easily see that item 2 is true: Ghosts *have* been reported throughout history. We can probably verify item 1 just as easily. Remember, these statements alone do not prove that ghosts are real; these statements are just one bit of evidence that might support that idea. We have to decide whether it is significant that people throughout history and of all ages have reported seeing ghosts.

Ideally, the author should tell us the source of any statement of fact so that we can confirm it. But many authors simply expect the reader to take their word for it. Be careful not to accept something as a fact just because the author has stated it.

Implied logical reasoning (item 2). Authors often use examples of logical reasoning to lead the reader to the author's desired conclusion. Here is an example:

> Several people in this article had comforting experiences with ghosts. Therefore, ghosts provide comfort to the living.

This seems pretty logical. The danger is that sometimes what seems logical really is not. A logical fallacy is when something appears to be logical but really is not. Here's an example: I have never seen a ghost, therefore ghosts do not exist. This is a fallacy because it is an overgeneralization. There are a lot of things you have not experienced that are real. For instance you have not experienced spaceflight, the bubonic plague, or death, yet all exist.

Another kind of logical fallacy is a false analogy, in which you wrongly compare two things based on a common quality. Here is an example:

> Dogs wag their tails when they are happy. Cats that wag their tails must be happy, too.

The fallacy is that cats and dogs are different species. In fact, a cat wagging its tail may be angry, indecisive, or ready to pounce on prey. Cats do not typically wag their tails when they are happy. Here is another example of a logical fallacy:

> My sister's Toyota Celica lasted for 250,000 miles. I want a car that will last a long time, so I am going to buy a Celica, too.

The fallacy here is that your sample is too small. There are millions of Celicas on the road, and you are basing your judgment on one of them. Two hundred fifty thousand miles may be typical—or it may be very unusual. Before you make a buying decision, you need to get more information to determine the average lifetime mileage for a Celica.

Implied logical thinking is when the author states part of the argument and leaves you to figure out the rest. In the La-

Grand article, the author tells us that a stigma is attached to reporting unsubstantial things like ghosts. The author does not state it, but he implies (wants you to assume) that because of the stigma, people would not make up such things. Therefore, if they report them they must be true. What do you think—is item 3 logical thinking or a logical fallacy?

Expert or celebrity testimonial (items 5 and 6). Many writers support their claims with testimony from an expert or a celebrity. A lot of television ads do this. You have probably seen the famous young golfer Tiger Woods in commercials selling cars, shoes, and food products, and you likely have seen medicine commercials in which doctors tell the benefits of that product. Advertisers know that many people are influenced when a celebrity or expert says something is true. Article writers know this as well.

Celebrity testimony usually does not have much value as evidence: If a celebrity likes a certain brand of shoes, does it mean the shoes fit well, are comfortable, and will wear well? Not necessarily. What it really means is that the celebrity's agent got the celebrity a certain amount of money to say that the shoes are good.

Celebrities are not just current music or movie stars. Any famous person could count as a celebrity in the sense we are using the term. Mary Todd Lincoln and Carl Jung, though long dead, count as celebrities. Because they are famous, we might consider their testimony more valuable than that of the other, unknown people in the article. In addition, Carl Jung is an expert. He was a famous psychologist who studied dreams and many other things relating to the human mind.

Some expert testimony can provide valuable evidence. In an article about car safety, a scientist who conducts experimental car crashes for the U.S. government can probably provide some valuable information. That is the key to expert testimony: The expert must be an expert on the topic under consideration, and the author must provide enough information so that you can judge whether this person is qualified to provide valuable information. Do you think the famous psychologist's report of seeing the ghost of a deceased colleague is good evidence?

Physical evidence (item 6). Physical evidence can be used to prove or disprove a hypothesis. In police cases, physical evidence includes things like fingerprints, DNA, murder weapons, and so on. Poltergeist cases generally have a lot of physical evidence, such as broken crockery and glassware and moved objects. Ghost cases are likely to have less physical evidence, although ghost investigators like Joshua P. Warren ("A Ghost Investigation") claim their instruments find evidence in the form of changed atmospheric conditions. In the LaGrand article, the author describes an instance when Jung found a different form of physical evidence: He envisioned a ghost in a library with a certain book. When Jung went to the actual library he found the book in the identical place it had been in his vision. Some skeptics might explain this by saying that Jung at some time must have seen this library or a photo of it and remembered it in the back of his mind. But Jung said he had not. What do you think—does Jung's experience support the idea of a ghost visitation?

4. Consider Alternative Hypotheses, or Explanations, for the Evidence

Once you have examined the types of evidence the author has provided and have considered how valuable the evidence is in supporting the author's claims, see whether the author has considered other possible explanations. If the author considers only one explanation for the evidence, he or she may be presenting a biased, or one-sided, view or may not have fully considered the issue.

LaGrand does briefly mention one alternative: Near the end of the article he states that critics say ghostly visitations are caused by the power of suggestion, but LaGrand does not examine this hypothesis. It would be helpful to have more information about the critics' perspective so you could evaluate for yourself whether this alternative hypothesis has any merit.

5. Draw a Conclusion About the Author's Claim

After considering the evidence and alternative explanations, it is time to make a judgment, to decide whether the hypothesis makes sense. You can tally up the evidence that does and does not support the hypothesis and see how many pros and cons you have. But that is really too simple. You will have to give more weight to some evidence than to others. Which of LaGrand's items of evidence seem most significant? Do they convince you that his hypothesis is true?

Exploring Further

Let's examine another article using hypothetical reasoning. Take a look at Joe Nickell's article "Ghostly Explanations." Perhaps the first thing to notice is that Nickell comes to this subject with a bias against it. He is a longtime member of the Committee for the Scientific Investigation of Claims of the Paranormal (CSICOP), an organization that is vocally skeptical about paranormal, including ghostly, claims. However, Nickell is also an experienced investigator. As you read his article, you should try to decide if he has put aside his bias and has treated the subject as objectively as possible.

Now let's review Nickell's article using the steps for hypothetical reasoning.

1. State a Hypothesis

Here is one possible hypothesis for Nickell's article: Ghostly phenomena have common explanations.

2. Gather the Author's Evidence

This article covers several different kinds of ghostly phenomena and thus contains a lot of different kinds of evidence. Here is some of it:

1. The author quotes several experts, including psychologist Robert A. Baker, psychic researcher Nandor Fodor, and others.
2. The author states that there was no report of a ghost in Liberty Hall until the 1930s, even though the ghost was said to have been from 1817.
3. The witness who described the Liberty Hall ghost was "an impressionable and apparently quite emotional schoolgirl (who remained unmarried until her death in 1934 and who dabbled in fortune-telling and similar occult pursuits)."
4. The ghost was "just the type of image a young Victorian lady would have conjured up."
5. The author cites the results of an investigation of ghostly lights in a home that turned out to be car lights reflected in a mirror.
6. The author provides some anecdotes (little stories), including a personal account, showing how ordinary lights can be mistaken for ghosts.
7. In the section called "Phantom Footfalls," the author describes his own investigation of ghostly noises at MacKenzie House, a famous haunted house in Toronto.
8. In the section called "Haunted Rocking Chair," the author lists several simple causes of mysterious chair rocking, including the wind and an unstable floor.

9. In the section called "Ghostly Door," the author quotes an eyewitness who was a self-identified skeptic and who, over fifteen years, never saw a door move mysteriously despite the many reports from others that it had done so.

10. The author reports his discoveries about a supposed haunted mill, including explanations for mysterious door banging and ghostly blood. The investigation included forensic (scientific laboratory) examination of the substance thought to be blood.

11. In the section called "Phantom Hitchhiker," the author says that this is a "century-old tale that well illustrates the human desire for legend making."

12. The author quotes psychologist Robert A. Baker, who says, "We tend to see and hear those things we believe in."

3. Examine the Evidence

In this article, Nickell uses many kinds of evidence, including expert testimony (items 1 and 12), statements of fact (item 2), implied logical thinking (item 2 and 11), ridicule and innuendo (items 3 and 4), physical evidence (items 5, 7, 8, and 10), anecdotal evidence (item 6), and eyewitness testimony (item 9). Let's look at some of this evidence.

Expert testimony (items 1 and 12). Writers who are researchers, investigators, and scholars tend to cite a lot of experts who can help bolster their case. It is sometimes helpful to look up the original information to find out more about what the cited expert says about the topic. Some authors do not provide source information; they simply name the expert. But most serious researchers, investigators, and scholars provide full source information in footnotes or a text note so that the original source can easily be found. Joe Nickell did originally include such information, but it was omitted here for easier reading.

Review the information about expert testimony in the section on the LaGrand article, then decide if Nickell's use of expert testimony supports his hypothesis.

Statements of fact (item 2). Review the information on statements of fact, then decide if item 2 supports Nickell's thesis.

Implied logical thinking (items 2 and 11). Review the information on implied logical thinking in the section on La-Grand's article.

In item 2, Nickell doesn't say explicitly, but he implies that if there were really a ghost from 1817, there should have been reports before the 1930s. In item 11 Nickell implies that because phantom hitchhiker tales exemplify the "human desire for legend making," that explanation ought to be considered for ghost reports in general. Do you think these two examples are logical thinking or logical fallacies?

Ridicule and innuendo (items 3 and 4). Also known as name-calling, ridicule and innuendo make fun of or belittle something in order to decrease its credibility. In general, this is not a useful kind of evidence. An author often uses this as a substitute for real evidence. You must read carefully to see if any evidence is behind the ridicule.

In item 3 Nickell tells us that the witness was impressionable and emotional. He adds that she never married and she dabbled in the occult. Parts of this description may be simple statements of fact: If she indeed "ran screaming from the room," she was certainly emotional at the time she claimed to see the event, but Nickell does not provide enough information for us to judge whether the witness was typically an emotional person. By describing her in this way, Nickell is suggesting that she is not rational and therefore not a good witness.

The information that she never married seems to have little to do with whether she saw a ghost, but the information that she dabbled in the occult could be very relevant. On one hand, it could be considered belittling information: Many readers would find this information off-putting and think the witness was superstitious and therefore not a good witness. But if the statement is true, the fact that she was interested in the occult may mean that she was predisposed to see a ghost.

Item 4 is also belittling. It suggests that the witness relied on a Victorian stereotype and thus is not good evidence of an actual occurrence.

You decide: Is Nickell's description of this witness and what she saw simple reporting? Is it objective? Does it provide convincing support for his hypothesis?

Physical evidence (items 5, 7, 8, and 10). Nickell uses lots of physical evidence in his discussion; he reports on the results of his own and others' investigations looking for evidence or examining alleged evidence of ghostly visitations.

Some investigators use high-tech instruments in their investigations. For example, Joshua P. Warren, in the article "A Ghost Investigation," uses many kinds of scientific instruments to discover varying temperatures, electromagnetic effects, and other changes in atmospheric conditions to prove that something unusual is occurring. Skeptics, also, might use such equipment to show that nothing exceptional happened. In fact, Nickell tells us that he used a scientific laboratory to verify that some ghostly "blood" was actually not blood at all.

Many times, however, simple observation and experimentation with ordinary forces are enough for an investigator to solve a case. In this article, Nickell and the experts he cites rely primarily on simple explanations. Nickell shows us how lights reflecting from mirrors or other surfaces can appear to be ghost lights, how a breeze can cause a chair to rock mysteriously, how sound can echo from a next-door building to give the effect of ghostly footfalls, and so on. As you read, your job is to think about the physical evidence that Nickell provides and decide if it is good supporting evidence for his hypothesis.

Anecdotal evidence (item 6). An anecdote is a brief story. An eyewitness report is one example of anecdotal evidence. Authors use anecdotes to illustrate a point or to make an analogy. For instance, Nickell uses the anecdote about his own experience with the "old man" by the side of the road to show how easy it is for our senses to be fooled.

Anecdotal evidence contrasts with hard evidence (which includes such things as facts, physical evidence, and statistical evidence), which investigators usually consider more significant than anecdotal because it is easier to prove or disprove. However, anecdotal evidence can sometimes be very strong, especially when there are multiple sightings of the same thing.

Eyewitness reports (item 7). See the information about eyewitness reports in the section on LaGrand's article, then decide if this eyewitness report is good supporting evidence for Nickell's hypothesis.

4. Consider Alternative Hypotheses

Does Nickell consider alternatives to his hypothesis that ghostly phenomena have simple explanations? Can you think of alternative hypotheses he should have considered?

5. Draw a Conclusion

You decide: Does Joe Nickell make a good case for his hypothesis? What evidence most influences your decision?

Other Evidence

Statistical or numerical evidence. Authors also use types of evidence other than the ones described above. One important type is statistical or other numerical data. When deciding whether something happened by chance or on purpose, statistics can be very important. Authors also sometimes use numbers to show that a large number of people believe something or have experienced something. High numbers might convince some readers that the author's hypothesis is true. Evaluate all numerical claims carefully. Where did the numbers come from? If they are from a survey, how old is the survey? What do the numbers really mean?

Statements of opinion. A statement of opinion cannot be proven true or false—it is simply what someone believes. (Statements of opinion often are based on or contain factual statements that can be verified. For example, "I think you are angry" is a statement of opinion, but it can be verified when your face turns red and you hit me in the nose.)

Whether we accept a statement of opinion as good supporting evidence depends on the nature of the opinion and what we think of the person giving it. For example, if our history teacher says, "Peace in the Middle East will not happen for a very long time," we may accept that as evidence because we respect that teacher's knowledge about world events. But if the same teacher tells us, "Fashion models will be wearing white socks with their black trousers next year," we may be less inclined to take this opinion seriously unless he or she clearly keeps up with the latest fashion trends.

If an author relies heavily on opinion, you must decide if the author—or his sources—are reliable.

Now You Do It!

Choose one article from this book that has not already been analyzed and use hypothetical reasoning to determine if the author's evidence supports the hypothesis. You can use the following form.

Name of article_____ Author_____

1. State the author's hypothesis.

2. List the evidence.

3. Examine the evidence. For each item you have listed under #2, state what type of evidence it is (statement of fact, eyewitness testimony, etc.) and evaluate it: Does it appear to be valid evidence? Does it appear to support the author's hypothesis?

4. Consider alternative hypotheses. (What alternative hypotheses does the author consider? Does he or she consider them fairly? If the author rejects them, does the rejection seem reasonable? Are there other alternative explanations you believe should be considered? Explain.)

5. Draw a conclusion about the hypothesis. Does the author adequately support his or her claim? Do you believe the author's hypothesis is valid? Explain.

Glossary

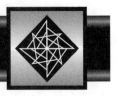

apparition: A supernatural appearance of a person, animal, or other creature.

crisis apparition: A person's spirit or ghost that appears to another at a time of extreme crisis; for example, at a man's moment of death his spirit may appear to his mother.

demon: A spiritual entity usually thought to be connected to the Devil or Satan; not a ghost.

ghost: A spirit of a dead person that manifests in some way so the living can perceive it.

hallucination: An apparition caused by physical or mental illness, drugs, or a susceptible mental condition such as the groggy state a person experiences upon awaking.

haunting: An apparition that appears (or is sensed in some other way) repeatedly over an extended period, possibly decades or even centuries; associated with a particular place.

medium: A person who is able to contact spirits for others; also called a psychic, reader, or channeler.

paranormal: "Beyond the normal"; things that cannot be explained by scientific means.

parapsychology: The study of the paranormal.

poltergeist: "Noisy [or mischievous] spirit"; baffling incidents of objects flying around a room or crashing to the ground, erratic electrical events (such as lights turning on and off, telephones ringing), and even physical effects (such as the appearance of scratches and welts), all without apparent cause but related in some way to a focus person, often a preadolescent, an adolescent girl, or a person repressing extremely strong emotions.

RSPK: Recurrent Spontaneous Psychokinesis; recurring incidents of a person causing things to happen through mental power alone; considered by some to be the explanation for poltergeists.

For Further Research

Loyd Auerbach, *Mind over Matter*. New York: Kensington Books, 1996.

Dawn Baumann Brunke, "Interview with a Ghostbuster," *FATE*, October 1995.

Andy Coghlan, "Midnight Watch," *New Scientist*, December 19, 1998.

Perry DeAngelis and Steven Novella, "Hunting the Ghost Hunters," *The Connecticut Skeptic*, Summer 1997. www.theness.com.

Hazel Denning, *True Hauntings: Spirits with a Purpose*. St. Paul: Llewellyn Publications, 1996.

Hilary Evans, "The Naked Ghost," *The Anomalist*, Winter 1995.

Hilary Evans and Patrick Huyghe, *The Field Guide to Ghosts and Other Apparitions*. New York: Quill, 2000.

William G. Everist, "Bisbee Bed and Breakfast," *FATE*, September 1996.

Edith Fiore, *The Unquiet Dead: A Psychologist Treats Spirit Possession*. New York: Ballantine, 1988.

Vincent H. Gaddis, *Mysterious Fires and Lights*. Garberville, CA: Borderland Sciences Research Foundation, 1994.

Rosemary Ellen Guiley, *The Encyclopedia of Ghosts and Spirits*. 2nd ed. New York: Checkmark Books/Facts On File, 2000.

Hans Holzer, *America's Restless Ghosts: Photographic Evidence of Life After Death*. Stamford, CT: Longmeadow, 1993.

Dennis Houck, *The National Directory of Haunted Places: Ghostly Abodes, Sacred Sites, UFO Landings, and Other Supernatural Locations.* New York: Penguin, 1996.

J. Michael Krivyanski, "Probing the Phenomena Called Ghosts," *World and I,* August 2001.

Louis E. LaGrand, *After Death Communication: Final Farewells.* St. Paul: Llewellyn Publications, 1997.

Randolph Liebeck, "Going After Ghosts?" *FATE,* April 1997.

Raymond Moody, *Reunions: Visionary Encounters with Departed Loved Ones.* New York: Ivy Books, 1993.

Lance Morrow, "A Mystic of Houses," *Time,* June 30, 1997.

Joe Nickell, *Entities: Angels, Spirits, Demons, and other Alien Beings.* Amherst, NY: Prometheus Books, 1995.

Michael Norman and Beth Scott, *Haunted America.* New York: Tor, 1994.

Katherine Ramsland, *Ghost: Investigating the Other Side.* New York: Thomas Dunne Books/St. Martin's, 2001.

James Randi, "The Columbus Poltergeist Case: Flying Phones, Photos, and Fakery," in *The Outer Edge: Classic Investigations of the Paranormal.* Ed. by Joe Nickell, Barry Karr, and Tom Genoni. Amherst, NY: Committee for the Scientific Investigation of Claims of the Paranomal, 1996.

Bertram Rothschild, "The Ghost in My House: An Exercise in Self-Deception," *The Skeptical Inquirer,* January 2001.

Richard Southall, "Ghostbusting on a Budget," *FATE,* October 1997.

Philip Stander and Paul Schmolling, *Poltergeists and the Paranormal: Fact Beyond Fiction.* St. Paul: Llewellyn Publications, 1996.

Brad Steiger, *Shadow World: Spiritual Encounters That Can Change Your Life.* New York: Signet, 2000.

Troy Taylor, *The Ghosthunter's Guidebook.* Alton, IL: Whitechapel Productions, 1999.

G.N.M. Tyrrell, *Apparitions.* New York: Collier Books, 1953.

Ed and Lorraine Warren with Robert David Chase, *Ghost Hunters: True Stories from the World's Most Famous Demonologists.* New York: St. Martin's, 1989.

Joshua P. Warren, "In Search of the Pink Lady," *FATE,* June 1997.

Michael White, *Weird Science: An Expert Explains Ghosts, Voodoo, the UFO Conspiracy, and Other Paranormal Phenomena.* New York: Avon, 1999.

Richard Williams, ed., *Quest for the Unknown: Ghosts and Hauntings.* Pleasantville, NY: Reader's Digest Association, 1993.

Colin Wilson, *Poltergeist: A Study in Destructive Haunting.* St. Paul: Llewellyn Publications, 1993.

Patty Wilson, "The Haunted U.S. Hotel," *FATE,* October 2001.

Index

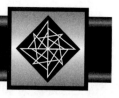